TEMPTING *Teacher*

Decadent Temptations
Book Four

MICHELLE WINDSOR

This one is for Lydia Michaels.
For teaching me so much more than writing.
For restoring my faith in friendships.
And for always being there for me.

Chapter One

~Alexander~

"How much?"

"For?"

"Don't try and be coy with me, Xander."

Her painted lips pursing into a tight smile as one perfectly sculpted brow arches.

She was right. I was being coy. And why not? It came with the territory. I knew exactly what she wanted, but sometimes making them come right out and ask for it was so much more fun. For me, of course. I swing my legs out from under the table, then cross one knee over the other. I bring the tumbler of whiskey I'm holding to my mouth and take a very slow sip, my eyes never leaving hers. I swallow, run my tongue across my lower lip to capture every bit of the savory liquid, and of course, to tease her. "Are you asking how much longer our date is?"

"No." Her manicured nail taps against the stem of her champagne flute, then stops. "How much for you to fuck me?"

"Ah, that." I cock one side of my mouth up, enjoying the flush that colors her cheeks. I decide I want to make her squirm just a bit more. "You understand that Temptations is a reputable escort agency? That you hire an escort to take you to dinner, or a ball perhaps, or maybe even to an awards show?" I take another taste of my drink, and continue to toy with her. "Have the contracts changed to include sexual favors?" I force a frown, shaking my head. "Someone has some explaining to do at Temptations."

"Stop trying to embarrass me." She hisses from across the table, leaning her body closer as she lowers her voice. "Marjorie Perkins said you might, said that you, that-"

I close the distance between us, my face now an inch from hers, and finish the sentence she can't seem to complete. "That I might fuck you for the right price."

Her eyes widen as she draws a sudden breath through flared nostrils, her exhale hot when she responds. "Yes."

I shift my gaze to her mouth, her bottom lip currently clenched between her teeth, her red lipstick smearing. I love that she's nervous. Most of the women that pose this question don't even bother to ask. They simply assume. She's certainly beautiful enough to make my dick hard. Fucking her wouldn't be a hardship. But still, I want to know more. I was so tired of dates requesting I tie them up or spank them so they can live out some god damn fantasy they watched in a movie. I admit, at first, it was fun, but after a while, anything can get old.

And let's be extra clear; taking money for sex is illegal in the state of New York. The agency I work for, Temptations, isn't involved, or have knowledge of, these transactions in any way. Any risk I take in accepting or considering an offer like this is mine completely.

I reach out and use my thumb to tug her lip free, then swipe the pad against her teeth to remove the stain. "Aren't you married Jessa? What aren't you getting at home that you need from me?"

"Honestly?"

"That would be a nice change of pace." I muse out loud.

"My husband has been screwing his secretary every Friday night for the past several months." She huffs, rolling her eyes. "Yes, I know, so original of him, right?"

I shrug, not sure if she really needs a response. "Ah, so you want to get even." It's a declaration, not a question.

"Does that make me an awful person?"

"I don't really think I'm in any position to judge. I fuck people for money." Let's also be clear; I never said I followed the law.

"You'll do it then?" Hope blossoms across her features.

"What exactly do you want me to do?" I lean back, uncrossing my legs as I toss back the rest of my drink.

"I have a room reserved here. On the fifteenth floor. It faces my husband's office. He's working there right now. I want you to have sex with me in the window. I want him to see. I want him to get a taste of his own medicine."

"Twenty-five hundred. Two hours. I'll fuck you anywhere you want, anyway you want, in any hole you want."

Her mouth forms a small O shape at my words, silence the only sound between us.

"To answer your original question of how much." I lift my hand to flag the waiter for the check. "Plus, the cost of dinner of course."

"Okay." She stammers, pulling a black American Express card from an Hermes wallet that I'm sure cost more than most people's monthly rent. She slides it into the leather binder the waiter left, raising her eyes to mine. "I'm assuming cash works best?"

"Cash is all that works." I place my hand over her trembling one. "Are you sure you want to do this?"

"Yes." She shifts her gaze to our joined hands, a nervous laugh tumbling from her. "No."

I lift my hand and place it under her chin, raising it until she's looking at me. "This is all about you. I'll only do what you want. Nothing more. You're in control here. I promise there is nothing to be scared of. At least, not from me."

"What if he doesn't even care?" Her voice is barely a whisper. "Then what do I do?"

"Then you have a different decision to make. One that I can't make for you." The waiter discreetly swipes the binder off the table, trying not to disturb us. "But I can promise you this, Jessa; between now and then, I'm going to make sure the only thing you think about is how good my cock feels inside of you."

"Oh!" Her cheeks turn a lovely shade of pink, and I can't help but wonder if her nipples are the same shade. Yes, that's the kind of guy I am. What did you expect? You got the part where I fuck for money, right?

Ten minutes later she inserts a key card into the door of the room she's reserved. Once we're inside, she walks straight across the room to the full-size windows and pulls the curtains back until they are wide open. She lets out a small huff and then points. "There he is." Her head shakes back and forth. "I think I hate him."

I walk up behind her, looking over her head to where she's pointing. "Good, it will make this easier."

She spins around. "Do I pay you now?"

"Generally, after, but whatever makes you comfortable."

"I want to pay you now." She yanks her purse open to pull her wallet out. She extracts a wad of bills, all hundreds, and starts counting, then hands me the stack. "Twenty-five hundred."

"Just happened to have that on you?" I murmur, folding the bills before slipping them into the inside pocket of my jacket.

"Well, Marjorie gave me a general idea of what to have with me."

"Isn't she helpful?" I smirk, shrugging the jacket off, folding it over a nearby chair. Her eyes follow me, but no other part of her moves. "How do you want to do this?"

"Can you just tell me what to do?" Again, with the lovely shade of pink on her cheeks.

"As in, you want me to take control, or you want me to walk you through what we can do?"

She shuffles her feet, her lip clenched between her teeth again as she nods.

I take three steps, stopping when I'm in front of her, and gently pry her purse from her fingers, setting it on the table next to her. "I need you to tell me which one."

"Just take control." She peeks up at me from under her long lashes. "It's been so long I'm not even sure I remember how to do this anymore."

What a fucking idiot her husband is. This woman is beautiful, and seems to be kind, and for some insane reason, still in love with him. No matter how much she tries to proclaim otherwise. I thread my fingers through her silky auburn strands to wrap a hand around her head, then tilt it back as I lower my lips to hers. I start slow, feathering kisses against the corners of her mouth, the top, and then the bottom before finally covering it entirely. When she parts her lips in a small sigh, I take advantage, sweeping my tongue inside, tasting her, shoving it deep when she opens further. Her arms latch around my neck, and she arches her body to mine, a small groan escaping from her.

I find the zipper on the side of her dress and pull it down, one click at a time, then slide my hand inside, pressing my fingers against her back to tug her even closer. She surprises me by drawing away, my hand coming free as she retreats a step, her chest rising and falling in time to the small pants escaping her.

Before I can ask what's wrong, she brings her fingers

to the buttons of my shirt and begins working them. She glances up at me for less than a second then focuses back to her task. I don't object. This is her party. I'm more than happy to give her what she wants. I help, untucking my shirt from my pants, releasing the buttons that had previously been hidden. I unfasten the cuff links at each wrist, twisting to place them on the nearby table, then face her again. She spreads her hands wide under the shirt, placing them flat on my chest, gliding them up over my shoulders until the material falls down my arms to the floor.

"My God, you're stunning." Her hands continue to explore my torso, tracing over my skin as she stares up at me. "You almost hurt to look at with your clothes on, but this is more than I could have imagined."

"Let's see if you look as good as I imagined." Before she can react, I reach down, grab the hem of her dress and tug it over her head. Fuck me. She's wearing garters. So fucking old school. Her bra and panties are made of a sheer black silk fabric that leaves nothing to the imagination, and my cock stiffens in delight.

"You're fucking sexy." I snag a hand around her waist hoisting her flush, making sure she can feel just how good I think she looks.

A small yelp sounds when she lands against my length, and I slam my mouth to hers, devouring her moans as I grind myself against her core. Her fingers somehow wedge their way between us to release the buckle of my belt, and then the button of my slacks. She moves her mouth against mine as she pleads for me to take them off. I comply, releasing her to remove my shoes and then my pants.

She surprises me as she reaches to wrap her fingers around my girth through my briefs. "I thought you didn't remember how to do this." I practically growl as her grip tightens and begins to rub up and down my length.

"I guess it's like riding a bike." She purrs, looking up at me, her hair tousled and falling across her eyes.

"Oh honey, I can guaran-fucking-tee you that this is going to be so much better than riding a bike." I yank her closer, my fingers moving to her back, releasing the clip on her bra with one swift flick, stripping it from her with another flick. Sweet pink nipples. Just like I imagined. Small and so fucking perfect as they point up at me, begging to be sucked. I latch onto one without another thought, pulling hard, then lick the hard tip back and forth, my arm wrapped around her waist as she grinds her core against my thigh, wetness spreading over my skin each time she moves.

I pop my mouth off her breast, cradle her waist with my hands and lower to my knees. I slip my fingers under the waistband of her panties and ease them down her legs. I peer up at her, locking my gaze with her lust filled one, and grin. "I'm going to eat your pussy now." I tap her foot, indicating she should step out of her undies, never breaking my hold on her. "I'm going to show you what it should feel like to be worshipped."

Before she can respond, I shove my hands between her thighs spreading them wide to draw her clit into my mouth. She's so damn wet I can't resist sliding a finger into her, my dick throbbing when she lets out a long groan. "Oh my God, Xander!" I swish my tongue back and forth, adding another digit, pumping in and out. I smile around her pussy when she tosses one leg over my shoulder, pressing herself harder into my face, rotating her hips against my hand. I plunge in faster, deeper, then bite on her clit, her orgasm exploding as her muscles clench around my fingers. A scream erupts as her knee buckle, the weight of her landing on my face, her hands clutching onto my shoulders. I stop when I feel the pulsing around my fingers cease, releasing the hold I have on her clit, swiping my tongue one last time over her center.

I rise, grabbing her waist to lift her, her leg sliding off my shoulder, stopping when my mouth finds hers. She moans when I slide my tongue inside, my cock jerking against her stomach when she sucks her own juices off my mouth. She's so fucking desperate to be loved. I want to kill her fucking husband for making her feel this way.

"That was so good. Too good." She murmurs resting her head against my shoulder, her arms wrapped around me.

"We're not done yet." I glance at the watch strapped to my wrist. "You still have another hour and forty minutes left on the clock."

She lifts her head, looking at me, her eyes wide. "I get more?"

"I think there's still the matter of your husband to address?" I remind her taking a step back to take my briefs off, my cock bouncing up against my navel. I can't hide the grin that stretches across my face when her eyes dart below my waist, her tongue darting out to swipe across her mouth. Oh, how I want her fucking mouth wrapped around me right now. But this is about her, so I shove that thought aside and get to work.

"Turn around and put your hands on the window." I order, bending down to retrieve a condom from my pants. She stares at me a moment, her brow furrowing.

"Do you want him to see you?" I motion with my chin in the direction of her husband's office.

The expression changes on her face, the furrow gone as she seems to remember the reason she is here. She nods once, then turns around and bends over, planting her hands against the glass. I almost fucking cum in the rubber as I slide it on. Her ass is fucking perfect. Some days I really do love my job. I strut up behind her, my cock grasped in one fist, and use my other hand to stroke her ass.

"Wait!" She straightens. "I want to make sure he doesn't miss this." She goes to her purse, reaches inside retrieving her cell.

"You can't record this." Folding my arms, my voice firm.

"Oh!" She halts. "That didn't even cross my mind." She holds her phone up. "I'm going to call the asshole and make sure he sees me."

I shrug my shoulders. I point to the window. "Resume the position then."

She obeys, keeping her phone clutched in one hand as she bends, leaning against the glass. This time, I don't waste any time, line up my cock, and thrust myself into her pussy in one shove. She lets out a moan, her muscles clenching around my dick like a vice.

"Do you want me to go slow, or hard and fast." I ask as I slide my cock almost all the way out and then plunge back inside in one hard motion. Her ass pushes against mine as I thrust, arching into my cock with force.

"Wait." She pants, then speaks again. "Siri, call Michael."

Oh shit, she wasn't kidding when she said she was going to call him. Siri responds in her robotic voice. "Calling Michael, mobile."

It rings only twice before he picks up. "Jessa."

"Mike."

I can't help myself, and drive into her again, harder this time, pleased when she grunts.

"Are you okay?"

"Never better." She lets out a small laugh. "Mike, this is for fucking that whore, Nancy."

"What? What the hell are you talking about?"

"Look out your window, you cheating bastard." She drops the phone, not hanging up, and then looks over her shoulder at me. "Fuck me, Xander, as hard as you can."

"You're the boss." I reach both of my hands around her chest to grab onto her tits. "Hold onto that fucking glass." And then I start. I slide in and then out, slow at first, driving deeper with each thrust until I'm pounding into her, her nipples squeezed between my fingers as I pinch. Her forearms are up on the window, her face sideways on the glass, her mouth hanging open as I hammer harder.

"He's watching, he's watching." She pants, her fingers clawing at the glass, her ass slamming back into mine each time I drive forward. She lets out a scream, her pussy convulsing around my cock, causing me to explode right after, sparks of light bursting under my closed eyelids as I milk every last bit of my release into the condom.

I ease out of her, pull the rubber off, throw it in the garbage, and then help her up. Her knees are shaking and I'm not sure if it's from fucking her or from the fact that her husband not only just watched, but heard her get fucked by another man. She twists in my arms, kisses me deeply, then flips her husband off.

Just another day at the office…

Chapter Two

"Are you sure this dress is okay?" I assess the simple white sun dress I'm in, then scan the outfit my cousin is wearing. It's a flowy pink, silk jumpsuit, with a silver belt, silver sandals, and more sparkling diamond jewelry than I'd ever seen.

"I promise, you look amazing." Serena disappears inside her walk-in closet for a moment, reappearing with several items. "Here, try these shoes, and put on this jewelry and you'll be fabulous."

I don't argue, because I honestly don't know any better, and at this point have to believe whatever she tells me. Serena, my older cousin, by only a year, has lived in New York City her entire life. Her family has never been ashamed of their wealth, and in fact, loves to flaunt it. With a huge apartment in the city, and what can only be called a small mansion in the Hamptons, her life is the opposite of mine. My parents, who have the same wealth as my cousin, chose to live in a much different way, raising my brother and I in the very quiet mountains of Vermont. We live in a lovely country house, on about thirty acres of land, which boasts a pond with ducks, and a barn with four horses, one cow and three goats.

We visited my cousin's family a total of four times in my twenty-three years. My parents were quite satisfied with the quaint lifestyle they led in the country and had no desire to leave it. I, on the other hand, was thrilled to be out of college and on my way to grad school, allowing me to finally have some freedom. I was spending the summer in the Hamptons with my cousin before starting school in the fall.

I finish lacing up the gold gladiator sandals, and then add gold hoops and a long matching chain. I check my reflection and agree the small touches change the mood of the outfit. I twirl in a circle, flashing a bright smile at my cousin. "Thank you! That definitely did the trick."

"Anytime." She grabs my hand and pulls me toward the hallway. "Now let's get down to the party!"

An hour later we're sitting at a table not far from the bar, sipping our third glass of champagne. My cousin's best friend, Allison, and another friend I just met tonight, Lily, are sitting with us. My cousin is busy pointing out who all the guests at the party are to me since I'm a complete fish out of water.

"Oh! There are the Sapphires; Drew and his wife Hannah." She discreetly points to a gorgeous couple speaking to my Aunt Sophia, Serena's mother, on the upper deck. "They own Sapphire Resorts. I think they might be richer than us." She giggles, then continues. "Mom and Hannah are friends, so if you ever need a place to stay that isn't my parents', they can hook us up with some killer rooms at one of their hotels."

"Sweet." I take a drink, admiring the couple.

"Too bad Drew's brother isn't here." She bumps her shoulder to mine while fanning her face dramatically. "Want to talk about tall, dark and oh so fuckable? He has tattoo's that will make your panties fall off."

"Benjamin?" Allison's brow arches, a mischevious smile lighting up her face in wonder.

"Yep, that's the one." Serena confirms.

"How come he wasn't invited?" I ask, my attention still on the Sapphires.

"He got married not that long ago." She snorts. "Some lucky bitch snagged him up, so I never see him out and about anymore." She smirks. "It's too bad cause I heard he was quite the player before he met her. Would have liked to have given that one a whirl."

"Down girl." I laugh, but stop abruptly when my eyes land on what may be the sexiest man I've ever seen appear on the large deck. "Speaking of hot, who the hell is that?"

"Who?" She follows the direction of my gaze. "Oh, him. Yum. He's definitely one fine specimen. Only one problem."

"Someone that good looking can not possibly have a

relevant problem." Lily chides, puckering her lips as she openly assesses him up and down.

I twist to face Serena. "What? Is he gay?"

"Maybe." She shrugs, draining her glass as she stares at him. "My mom hired him in attempt to make my dad jealous."

"What the hell does that mean?" My nose scrunches as I try to put one and one together.

"Mother Dearest is pretty sure that Daddy Dearest is having an affair with Natasha." She signals the bartender to bring us another round, but keeps talking. "See that red head that Mr. Sexy has his arm around?"

I nod, secretly wishing it was my back his hand was on.

"That is dad's secretary."

"Uncle Nick is sleeping with his secretary?" My eyes widen as my hand moves to cover my mouth, now hanging open in a very unladylike way.

"It wouldn't be the first time." One side of her mouth curving down. "Daddy seems to have a bit of a wandering eye."

"I'm sorry, Serena." I grab her fingers in mine to squeeze gently.

She sighs, looking back up at the stunning couple. "It is the first time I've actually see mother do something to try to fight back. Hiring someone that hot to keep Natasha away from daddy is pretty ballsy."

"So, wait?" I wave my hands in the air. "What do you mean, she hired him? Is he like, a gigolo?"

She snorts. "You're so damn cute with your country

lingo." She takes a long swig of the newly delivered champagne. "More like a prostitute I think."

"He's an escort." Allison states confidently. Three pairs of eyes swing in her direction as she continues. "It's true. He works for Temptations. It's a service in the city."

"So, he's going to have sex with her?" I practically shout in shock.

"Shhh, everyone will hear you." Allison giggles, the champagne clearly affecting her. "I mean, who knows, but I sure wouldn't kick that fine ass out of bed."

"But, what about your mom and dad, aren't you worried about them?" I tear my gaze away from the gorgeous gigolo, or whatever he is, to look at Serena.

"Whatever will be, will be. Nothing I do is going to change that, my sweet cousin." She jumps up out of her chair, swaying a bit. "Oh, look! There's Jeffrey and his friend, Colin. Let's go say hi."

I'm afraid my cousin won't make it across the lawn without stumbling into someone, or something, so I hook my arm through hers, as the four of us make our way to her brother, my cousin, Jeff. We spend an hour with them, at which point Serena is pretty wasted. Lily and Allison disappeared a few minutes ago with Colin to find a bath-room, so Jeff helps me bring her up to her room to put her to bed.

After she's settled, I decide to go down to the beach for a little quiet instead of back to the party. I follow the path on the outside perimeter of the lawn over a small wooden boardwalk. I relax into one of the Adirondack chairs posi-tioned at the edge of the beach. The moon is almost full, it's reflection on the white sand causing the night to look bright. The music of the party is barely audible over the lapping of the waves against the shore.

"Do you mind if I join you?" A deep voice startles me, a shriek escaping as I twist around, then freeze.

"Oh! It's you." I state, then realize I sound like a complete idiot.

"I'm sorry, have we met?" He steps closer, then bends down in front of me, analyzing me. "No, I think I'd remember someone as beautiful as you."

"Nice one. They teach you that in gigolo class?" I jest.

"What?" He scowls, rising to his full height, my head tilting back to keep eye contact with him. "I think I'll leave. Sorry if I disturbed you."

"Wait." I jump up from my chair, knowing what I said was not only out of line, but so out of character for me. "I'm sorry. Please, I shouldn't have said that. It was extremely rude."

The edges around his eyes crinkle when they narrow to look at me, one hand scrubbing his already tousled hair before one side of his mouth crooks up in a wicked smile. "Gigolo class? Want to explain what that was supposed to mean?"

"Nothing! Sorry!" I motion to one of the chairs. "Please, sit." I plop back into the seat I was previously in, hoping it will cause him to follow suit. "It was stupid, I shouldn't have said anything. Too much champagne."

He stares at me for a moment, but then, to my relief, he sits, shifting his attention to the water.

"I'm Summer, by the way." I rush out, trying to say something that won't make me look like a complete fool.

"Xander." He turns his face toward mine, extending his hand.

I take it, a small jolt of pleasure zinging through me when he turns it over to place a soft kiss inside my wrist. "Nice to meet you, Summer." He releases my hand, which hangs between us for a moment until I come to my senses and drop it back to my side.

"Xander with an X or with a Z?" I cock my head to one side, examining him further.

He chuckles, but humors me. "With an X. Why?"

"No reason." I shrug.

"No question is ever asked without a reason." He rises and lifts the chair, shifting it so it faces me, our feet now just a few inches apart. "Tell me. I want to know."

God, how did I get myself into these situations? I blow out a small sigh. "I was just curious."

"Go on." He prompts, not relenting. "Curious about what?"

"Just, well, I wondered what your mother must be like to name you Xander. It's such a super hero kind of name, or a name that you'd hear in a circus." Of course, now that I started, I can't seem to stop. "You know," I deepen my voice as I pretend to announce him. "Introducing Xander the Great!"

He stares at me, his face devoid of any emotion, and I start to squirm in my seat, fidgeting with the hem of my dress as I realize, once again, I just made an ass of myself.

I start to apologize, again, but he puts his hand up, shaking his head.

"Please, stop saying sorry." His brow furrows as he continues to peer at me. "You're a bit of an oddity, aren't you? Definitely not from around here."

I wonder if it's really that obvious. "No, I'm from Vermont. I'm visiting my aunt and uncle before I start school in the fall."

"Ah, well, I suppose that explains some of it." He scoots forward, his gaze intense as he scrutinizes me, murmuring his thoughts out loud. "You're quite innocent. Almost naive. You aren't being rude. You really just don't know."

I roll my eyes. "I know things. I'm not a complete moron."

His hand darts out and lands on my knee, another jolt of electricity sparking straight up my thigh to my core. I flinch, which seems to amuse him, because he chuckles. Instead of letting go, his fingers grip a little tighter. "I didn't say stupid. I said innocent. There's a difference."

I look down at his hand, and perhaps understanding he may have overstepped, his hold loosens, sliding off my leg as he leans back in his chair.

"Can I ask you another question?"

"Oh, I can hardly wait to hear what's going to come out of your mouth next." He chuckles. "Please, by all means, go ahead."

"Are you a prostitute?"

Chapter Three

~Xander~

"Fuck, you are definitely full of surprises, aren't you?" I throw my head back, barking out a laugh as I admire the moon above us.

"I'm sorry. I don't mean to offend you." She scoots forward in her chair. "It's just that Serena said that her mother hired you to, well, you know, keep my uncle's secretary busy tonight."

"You mean, Natasha?" I clarify.

She nods, but for once stays blessedly silent. I stare at her for several long moments, knowing she's uncomfortable when she starts to squirm in her seat. Putting her out of her misery, I continue. "The correct term is escort. I'm not a prostitute."

"But you take money to *be* with people." She counters,

my temper starting to flare just enough for my pulse quicken.

When I had noticed her earlier laughing with her friends, the way her face lit up sparked something inside of me I hadn't felt in ages. Natasha grew bored when Nicholas ignored her, so had called an Uber and left, giving me the perfect opportunity to follow this blonde mystery to the beach. Now I was beginning to wonder if I had made a mistake.

"I work for an agency that arranges dates for an event. Like the one here tonight. Or perhaps a dinner, or to the theater or a ballet. It's easier for people to have someone on their arm instead of going alone."

"And you have sex with them?" She persists.

"No." I blow out a sigh, clenching my hands together between my knees so I don't wrap them around her neck, then shrug. "Well, sometimes."

"So, you are a prostitute!" She declares in victory.

I close my eyes, pray for patience, then open them, her full lips stretched into a smile so breathtaking my heart skips a beat. I draw in a lung full of air, and am about to speak when she hops out of her chair and starts pacing back and forth.

"I have an idea but I don't know if you're going to like it, but I may never get a chance like this again, so if I don't ask, I'll always regret it, and then I will always wonder what could have happened if I had just asked, so I'm just going to ask." She rattles on, her words spewing out faster than I can digest, but when I do, I almost groan out loud at what I think she's going to ask me.

"No, I will not take your virginity." I announce before she has a chance to even ask.

"What?" She skids to a halt, sand springing up around her feet onto my Gucci loafers, her eyes popping wide as she leers down at me. "I am not a virgin."

"Really?" I laugh out loud. "I'm quite surprised, frankly."

"I've had sex." She stomps her foot down, crossing her arms over her tits, which I just happened to notice were peaked. "Almost twice."

"Almost twice?" I chuff. "You've either had someone's cock in you or you haven't. If you aren't sure, I'd hedge on the fact it's a no."

"Of course, I'm sure." She flops back into her chair again, heaving a loud sigh. "It was just fast. So, so fast." She shares, slapping a hand over her face. "It was barely in and then he came, and it was over and out."

"Twice." I hold two fingers up, trying not to laugh.

"Don't mock me." She huffs. "You have no idea what it's like growing up in a town with only twenty boys in your entire class. Most of them feeling like your brother because you've known them your entire life."

"How old are you?" I wonder out loud, hoping for my sake she's not just out of fucking high school.

"I'm twenty-three." She sighs, like she's ancient.

I exhale as well, in relief, knowing I still had some morals in not wanting to bed or be attracted to an eighteen-year-old. "And you didn't meet anyone in college?"

"That was in college!" She reveals, flinging a hand in the air. "And that's why I want to hire you."

"You want to what?" I repeat, not sure I heard her correctly. She stands again, but this time it's to move over to my chair, her small frame sitting on the wide arm, her body facing mine.

"I want to hire you." She licks her lips, her fingers rubbing together in her lap as she rushes on. "I want you to teach me how to do things a girl my age should know how to do by now."

"I'm too old for you." My voice firm.

"But experience is what I need, so you being older is perfect." She places a hand on my head and tilts my face into the light. "How old can you be anyway? You don't look older than thirty. And you're very attractive. You're the perfect person to teach me."

"No." I rise out of my chair, strolling several feet away from her, my heart racing at her proposal. Is she crazy? I'm not a sex instructor. I fuck. For money. And I'm good at it. I don't have to show or teach anyone what to do. I just do it. I spin to look at her. She's beautiful. Long blonde hair, a small petite frame, but with curves firm and tight due to her age. And her lips, fuck me if they aren't the first natural pair of puffy lips I've seen in years. They look soft as pillows instead of hard from endless shots of filler. Yes, if she had been any other socialite in the city, I would have already been on my way to her bedroom.

"Why?" She stands and takes a few steps closer to me. "Am I not attractive enough to be your client?"

"You might be too attractive." I mumble under my breath, and then say louder, "you're beautiful. This just isn't what I do."

She gets bolder and moves until she's right in front of me. "Do you know how to kiss someone?"

"Of course."

"Do you know what turns you on, what you like to do and what you like to have done to you?"

"Summer, I would destroy you." I invade her space now, wrapping a hand around her waist to haul her to my body, making sure she can feel my cock against her. I grab one of her hands to press it against my length, a gasp coming from her as I do. "Do you feel that? Do you know what I could do to you with this? How good it would feel for me to stick this into every hole in your body? Because that's what I want to do right now." I wrench her even closer, bring my lips just a breath away from hers. "Is that what you want?"

She nods her head, lifting her eyes to peek up at me, her lips brushing against mine when she answers. "Yes."

"Fuck!" I release her with a soft push, not expecting that reaction. "Why? Why not wait for the right guy to come along? Someone you love that will show you all these things. The right way. Not the dirty way you'd learn with me."

"I'm twenty-three years old, Xander." She lifts her shoulders, dropping them as she sighs. "A quarter of my life is over. I'm tired of waiting for the right guy. I want to take things into my own hands. And you can show me these things. Teach me. I don't want to find the right guy and then lose him because I don't even know how to give him a blow job."

"The right guy will show and tell you exactly what he needs."

"Right now, you're that guy. You can show me and tell me exactly what to do. I don't want to be this innocent little girl anymore."

I shake my head, not believing when I hear the words coming out of my own mouth. "You can't afford me."

Her head snaps up, hope blooming across her face. "I've got a ten-million-dollar trust fund that says I can."

Fuck. I'm out of options. I glare at her, unable to deny the idea is actually appealing to me. She's gorgeous. And I can't lie, her innocence is part of her appeal. To be able to know my cock would be the first she's ever sucked, or even better, to know my tongue would be the first one to taste her. My cock stirs at the thought, and I know I've already made up my mind, even if I haven't said it out loud yet.

"Five lessons. Two hours each. Two thousand a lesson."

Her mouth drops open, which does nothing to help my cock relax, instead thickening further. She jumps up and down, squeals in delight, then claps her hands before launching herself against my chest. "Thank you! Thank you!"

I pry her off of me before I decide to give her the first lesson right here on the beach. "I'm not your boyfriend. I'm not your friend. This is a job. I'll show you what you want, and then we're done. Okay?"

"Okay." She bobs her head.

"And Summer, I won't fuck you. That privilege should go to the right guy, not someone you pay."

"Oh." She frowns as if disappointed, but nods her understanding. "Okay."

I pull my phone out of my back pocket and open a new contact. "Give me your number."

"Uh, sure." She tells me the number and I enter it.

"What's your last name?" I shift my eyes to her.

"Knight. Summer Knight."

I stare back at her, a thousand thoughts running through my mind about her name, the irony of our entire situation in relation to it, but decide to keep them to myself. "I'll text you with a date and an address. You're going to have to come to the city. I don't have a place in the Hamptons."

"Oh, sure. That's fine." She continues to nod. "I can stay at my aunt and uncle's apartment."

"You pay the ten grand up front, at the beginning of the first lesson." God, why did I feel like such an ass dictating these terms to her? It's never bothered me before.

"Do you need it in cash, or can I Venmo you?" She doesn't seem to be bothered in the least with the details, so I guess that should make me feel a little better.

"It has to be cash. I can't exactly report this to the IRS."

"Oh yeah, of course." She laughs nervously. "That makes sense."

"Okay." I look over her shoulder at the water wondering if I'm making the biggest fucking mistake of my life, and then give her a final nod. "I'll text you. I'm going to take off."

"Yeah, okay." She swings her foot back and forth, making a wide arch in the sand. "I'll talk to you later then."

I nod, then turn to head back to the house. After only a couple steps, I twist my head. "My mother named me Alexander. Xander is the name I use for my work at Temptations. And my mother, she's amazing."

Chapter Four

~Summer~

Bolting upright in bed, my eyes dart to the clock on the nightstand to check the time. Blowing out a sigh of relief, I register it's only a little past ten. I tossed and turned almost the entire night; my mind unable to stop as I obsessed over what my first lesson with Xander would be like today.

I finally passed out around five, and must have slept hard because I feel like I just had a full night's rest. Perhaps the nervous energy fluttering around in my stomach was tricking my body into thinking it was well rested? In any event, it was time to get my butt in gear, so I throw the covers off and head to the shower.

I'm meeting Xander at two at his apartment, but still need to figure out what I'm going to wear, (*what does one wear to a sex lesson*), eat something and then go to the bank to get his payment. Ten thousand dollars. It's the first time I've ever used any money from my trust, and it's to learn about sex.

When I told Serena about my arrangement with Xander, I thought she would object and try to talk me out of it. She surprised the hell out of me though and didn't even blink twice at the idea. Her exact quote, "There's a hell of lot worse people you could learn from. You go, girl."

So, here I am, getting ready in the guest bedroom at my aunt and uncle's apartment in the city. Not really knowing what Xander planned on covering with me, I made sure all my bits were waxed the previous day, and gave my legs and underarms a fresh shave in the shower. I smooth on my favorite scented lotion and apply some cream to my face. I walk to the dresser, pull open a drawer and stare down at my panties.

I've never been one to wear sexy under garments. I wear what's comfortable, so my collection consists mostly of silk bikini bottoms and a few thongs that I'll wear only if the outfit absolutely requires it. I can certainly understand from a man's perspective why a thong is sexy, but to me, having a thin piece of material cutting into my butt crack all day sucks.

I doubt Xander will be getting into my pants today, or anytime soon for that matter, as he did state there would be no actual sex. I stop analyzing, grab a pair of the briefs and slide them on, a matching bra going on next.

Now for the hard part. What the hell do I wear? This isn't a date. But it's not like I'm going to a classroom either. If I throw on some cut-offs and a t-shirt, he might take that as too casual. If I throw on a sexy outfit, he may think I'm expecting more or that I'm treating this like a date. Which, for the record, I am not. In the end, I decide on a simple pink sundress and slide my feet into my favorite sandals. I run a brush through my long hair and decide to let it air dry. Giving myself a once over in the mirror, I nod in approval. Simple is usually better, right?

Three hours later, my heart hammering against my ribs, I raise my sweaty hand, clench it into a fist, and knock on his door. Less than a minute later the door swings open, Xander appearing in its frame. I take an unconscious step back, startled again by how handsome he is.

His gaze travels the length of my body before looking up at the ceiling, his head shaking back and forth. "Are you fucking kidding me?"

"What?" Glancing down, I run a hand over my dress checking to see if I spilled something.

"You look like a little girl in that dress, that's what." His hand sweeps between us like the offense of my outfit should be so obvious. "How am I supposed to treat you like a woman in that?"

"Oh, I'm sorry." My brows pinch together and I cross my arms. "Would you prefer I take it off? Then you can see that I am most definitely an adult."

"Keep your clothes on little girl." He lets out a low growl, yes, a growl, then wraps his hand around my bicep and pulls me into the apartment, slamming the door behind me. "I knew this was a bad idea."

Yanking my arm out of his grip to dig into my purse, I thrust a thick envelope at him. "Do you think ten grand in cash is a bad idea?"

"I think I should have charged you twenty." He sneers, dragging a hand through his dark locks, before snagging the money from my hand. Turning, he strolls away. "Come on."

My mouth hangs open a second before snapping shut as I scurry after him. He stops in front of a wide-open space that contains a living room and kitchen area. He spins around to face me and points to one of the couches. "You can sit there."

"Yes, sir." Mocking a salute as I move toward the seat.

Chuckling under his breath, he sits across from me, tossing the envelope of money onto a nearby table. "We're not playing that game today, but if we were, you'd already be over my lap with a pink ass."

My heart trips in my chest, my breath catching somewhere in my throat. Lowering myself until I'm sitting, I wonder if I heard him correctly. Glimpsing in his direction, I find him analyzing me with an intensity that sends a flush of goosebumps across my skin. I stare back at him, willing myself not to fidget, waiting for him to speak. When he finally does, I wish he hadn't.

"Tell me how you touch yourself." One leg crossing over the other as he leans back, his arms stretching out to rest along the back of the cushions.

"W-what?" My face heating.

"You heard me." His gaze traveling south to the area

between my legs. "How do you pleasure yourself? What do you do to make yourself feel good?"

Breaking from his gaze, I stare down at my clenched hands, speaking quickly. "I don't."

"What do you mean you don't?" Disbelief in his tone. "You don't masturbate?"

Clenching my fingers more tightly, I shake my head back and forth. "No."

"Ever?" His clothing rustles as he stands to stalk over to me, continuing to interrogate me. "You're telling me you never let your hand slide over your breasts then down between your legs to rub yourself?"

My head snaps up when I feel the cushion sag to my right. He's so close I can feel his body heat. I turn, swallowing the lump in my throat so I can speak. "No, I don't do that."

"Ever?" He repeats, like he just can't believe it's possible.

"Ever." I whisper.

"How are you supposed to know what you want if you don't even know what you like?" His voice softening.

"That's why I hired you, Xander." I blink over at him. "I need you to show me."

"Well, first things first." Reaching out to the coffee table, he grabs a remote and turns the television on. "Let's watch some porn and get you in the mood."

"Porn?" Uncertainty lacing the question.

"Please tell me you have at least watched porn."

Afraid to look him in the eye, I shake my head instead.

"Okay." He blows out a long breath. "What do you

like? Do you know what excites you? A girl with another girl? Sex in the shower? Maybe sex with a stranger?"

Biting onto my bottom lip, I shrug my shoulders and gape at the large screen on the wall, every sex category you can think of listed in a menu. "They have man on man sex on this?"

"Yes. And women with women, and sometimes two men with one woman, and sometimes a bunch of men with one woman." He hands me the remote. "Pick one."

"Have you slept with a man before?" I blurt out, fixing my eyes on him.

"Yes." He states plainly.

"Have you slept with more than one woman at a time?"

"Yes." He repeats.

"Have you slept with men and women at the same time?"

"Yes." He deadpans, clearly bored with this line of questioning.

My brows rise as I ingest this. "Are you gay?"

He chuckles. "I'm me. I don't label myself. If I'm attracted to someone, then I act on it." He shifts so he's facing me. "But this isn't about me. This is about you. Can you tell me one time you were attracted to someone? Or someone that you dreamed about or had a fantasy about?"

Closing my eyes, I try to push down the embarrassment thrumming through me as I share the one fantasy I've had over and over since my sophomore year of college. "There was a professor at the University. He was beautiful. I would sit in class and wish that he would ask to see me after class in his office. And when I went, he would shut the door, lock it, then kiss me before taking me on his desk from behind."

Peeking my eyes open, I peer over to Xander, my cheeks flaming at my admission, his gaze dark and penetrating. His tongue sweeps across his lips, leaving a glistening wetness in its wake. My blood swooshes through my veins as we lock eyes as I wonder if he's going to kiss me. His deep voice startles me when he speaks. "So, you have a naughty teacher fetish?"

As if it's even possible, my cheeks got even hotter. "Well, no, not a fetish. It's just a fantasy. I've never done it before. It was just something I thought of once."

Surprising me, he lets out a chuff of laughter. "Relax little girl. I'm only teasing you. I can work with the teacher fantasy."

He takes the remote from my fingers, presses a few buttons, then sets it down. A second later the screen changes and a movie starts. My attention shifts when Xander rises and moves to the other side of me and sits, pressing his back against the arm of the couch. "I want you here." His grip fastens around my waist, turning my body so that my back is wedged between his legs. Before I can ask why, hot breath blows against my ear as he murmurs into it. "I'm going to show you how to touch yourself."

Heat cascades down my body, gathering directly between my legs and I wonder if I'll even need to watch what's on. But I do. I lift my head and take in the scene unfolding on the screen. It's a girl, dressed in a short plaid skirt and white oxford shirt, tied at her waist of course, and she's writing on a chalkboard; "*I will not pass notes in class*" over and over again. The teacher is sitting at his desk, pretending to grade papers, but can't seem to stop looking at the girl. Of course, she notices, and coyly drops the chalk, bending down to pick it up, exposing the fact that she's only wearing a thin scrap of string between her legs. The teacher tries to rub his penis discreetly, at which point she offers to help him, and the next thing you know, his dick is in her mouth.

"How does that make you feel?" His voice vibrates against my hair. I shift, and when I do, feel his hard length against my ass, a zap of electricity shooting straight to my core. "Keep watching." He whispers, covering my hand with his, sliding it up my thigh until it's under the material of my dress.

My chest rises and falls as my breath starts to come out in little pants. He drags my fingers over the damp silk covering my center, pressing down when we reach my clit. I jerk into him, his cock digging against the crack of my ass, a low moan escaping me. He takes my other hand and guides it over one of my breasts, the nipple erect and hard, even through the cotton. He squeezes my hand, forcing me to pinch the tip, the pain exquisite as it slices straight through me.

My head falls back against his chest, my lids closing as I try to soothe the ache throbbing between my thighs, stroking more quickly. Xander moves my hand to slide it under the hem of my underwear until my fingers brush against my smooth skin, gasping when I feel how wet I am. He forces my fingers deeper, parting my folds until I'm rubbing against my clit, my legs splaying wide.

"You're so fucking wet." He purrs, his dick throbbing against my backside. "Does this feel good?"

"Yes." I pant, my hair sliding over his chest as I nod emphatically. "It feels good." I pinch my nipple without his prompting, savoring the sweet agony it brings, the fingers at my core increasing the pressure as they stroke like lightening again and again over my clit.

I realize that Xander is no longer guiding my movements and is instead cradling me in his lap, his lips brushing against my ear as he whispers how well I'm doing. Spinning higher and higher, I grab my nipple between two of my fingers and squeeze, twisting it as I plunge two fingers inside myself. My entire body clenches, and I explode, a scream erupting from my lungs. My pussy spasms around my hand as I grind it deeper, white sparks bursting beneath my eyelids as I ride out my very first orgasm.

As I float back to consciousness, I slide my fingers free from between my legs, small convulsions fluttering like butterfly wings inside my core. I clench my thighs together in an attempt to prolong the pleasure, a breathy groan slipping through my lips as I feel my body relax against Xander's hard one.

"Now that you know what that feels like, imagine how much better it will be with a hard cock inside of you." His voice is gravelly and low as his words reach my ears, jolting me back to reality.

I struggle to sit up, but he wraps his arms around me, keeping me flush to him. "No, don't run away. This is what you wanted to know from me, remember?"

I nod but stay silent as he continues. "You should know better than anyone what your body responds to and what it doesn't. What you want and what you don't. What excites you, or turns you off." He loosens his hold, but doesn't release me. "Your homework is to learn what that is. Watch some porn, buy some naughty books, go to a peep show downtown. That way, when you find someone you want to sleep with, you'll know what you want and won't be afraid to ask for it."

"Alright." I agree.

"Are you?" His tone softens. "Alright?"

"I'm a little angry." I admit, twisting in his arms to look at him.

"You think I was too rough?" His head tilts.

"No, not at all." I shake my head, smiling. "I'm mad that it took me this long to figure out how to do that to myself."

"Yes, well, let's hope I'm not creating a monster."

He pushes himself up, his crotch at eye level when he stands, making it impossible for me to not notice he's hard. I fixate on it for just a second then shift my gaze higher to find him leering down at me. "See something you like?"

"Does it hurt?" I wonder out loud.

"I'll survive." He holds a hand out to help me rise from the couch.

"Do you want me-" I stop short when I glance back to his face and see his features harden.

"Do I want you to what?" He steps into me, threading his fingers through the hair at the base of my scalp to tug my head back. "Suck my dick? Give me a hand job?"

His mouth is less than an inch from mine and for the second time today, I wonder if he's going to kiss me. I'm completely speechless. I continue to look up at him, blinking when he also stays silent. After what feels like minutes, but I know is only seconds, he bends, nips at my bottom lip, swipes his tongue over the sting and then releases me. I stumble back a step, my fingers moving to the spot on my mouth he bit, my eyes wide.

"We'll cover that in our next class." One side of his mouth crooks up. "Unless of course you've learned enough."

I narrow my eyes, then plaster on the biggest smile I can. "Just text me the day and time, Teach." I slide my sandals onto my feet, grab my purse, and then stride past him, pretending my heart isn't beating a thousand miles an hour in my chest.

"Be careful what you wish for little girl."

Chapter Five

~Xander~

As soon as the door slams shut, I march to the bathroom, shedding my clothes along the way. I twist the shower on, then step under, not waiting for the water to heat. I need something to douse the fire burning under my skin. I lift my face, sighing at the cool relief.

It does nothing to dull the ache in my groin however, which seems to serve as a throbbing reminder of what she just made me feel. As the water finally warms, I place one hand on the wall, and use the other to grip the base of my cock. Stroking my hard length, my eyes clench, the memory of her body against mine so fresh it only takes seconds for me to come.

"Fuck!" Roaring out my frustration, I rest my head in the crook of my arm. I cannot allow myself to develop feelings for this girl. She's a client, and can never be anything more. Feelings don't bode well for a man like me, and she certainly deserves someone a thousand times better. Rinsing clean, I turn off the water and step out of the shower. I wrap a towel around my waist, run a hand through my dripping hair, clenching my teeth as I realize I'm still fucking hard.

I wait almost two weeks to text her. I almost don't. But there are ten thousand reasons still sitting in a sealed envelope on my kitchen counter that persuade me. I knew she was getting worried. She had texted three times in the last five days asking about our next lesson. I was an asshole. I ignored every text. I needed space from her. Needed time to wrap a noose around any kind of feelings my heart seemed to think were possible with her. I choked that fucker out and now the only thing in the game was my head. Now, twelve days later, I was finally texting her back. "Ready for your next lesson?"

Her response was instant. She had no idea how to be coy. She just acted on impulse instead of playing games. Which of course, made her all the more attractive. The only way this was going to work, was if I did this at her place, not mine. I needed to be able to get the fuck up and out when our lesson was over. I sure as shit didn't need her scent on my couch, in my apartment, or anywhere near my bed. "Tomorrow. 4pm. Give me ur address."

"I'm staying at my uncle's apartment. I don't feel right doing that here."

Jesus fucking Christ with this girl. Nothing could be easy with her. I glance over at the envelope on the counter and consider it might be better to just return it. The devil on my shoulder feels differently though, a second later my fingers tapping out a reply. "Then find a place and send me the address. Otherwise, lesson is off."

This time her response isn't immediate. After staring at the phone for ten full minutes, I begin to wonder if she's changed her mind. A surge of disappoint washes over me, my reaction a little unexpected considering I'd made the decision to keep this entirely business. Even more surprising, the way my heart rate increases when she texts an hour later with an address.

The next day, promptly at four, an uber drops me off in front of the address she sent. Looking up at the building, sitting pretty on Fifth Avenue, directly across from the park, I wonder where the hell these people get their money. A doorman greets me as I approach, and I tell him I'm there to see Ms. Knight. He opens the door and directs me to the elevator, inserting a key below the floor numbers before pressing PH, and then stepping back out. "It will open directly into the apartment, Sir."

A few minutes later, the door slides open and I step into an empty foyer. "Hello?"

"In here." Her voice calls from the right, so I tread in that direction, meeting her in the hallway a short distance later.

"Hello." She clasps her hands in front of her, fidgeting with her fingers. "I see you found it okay."

"Your uncle's place?" My gaze travels the length of her, noting she opted for something more conservative this time, dressed in black capris and a loose, mint green tank top.

"My cousin actually." Her eyes dart over me, her cheeks flushing a light pink. Too fucking innocent. "Jeffrey. He's out at the Hamptons for the rest of the week."

"Where do you people get all your fucking money?" This time I muse out loud, as I scan the art work lining the hallway.

"Excuse me?" Her small hand lands at the base of her throat.

"A house in the Hamptons, this apartment, your trust fund, those diamonds in your ears." I cock my head. "Someone has a lot of money."

"Oh. Well." She shrugs. "My mother and my aunt are heirs to Erickson Energy."

My brow kicks up. Holy shit. That is one of the largest companies in the world. And she grew up buried in the country somewhere? "You're practically royalty." I state.

"No." She turns and beckons for me to follow. "I'm just a girl." She looks over her shoulder as she continues. "A little girl, according to you."

Noticing how good her ass looks as I trail behind her has me thinking otherwise at the moment, but I stay quiet. We enter a large open space containing a seating area, a dining room, and a kitchen fit for a five-star chef. Everything is decorated in gray and white, with black accents throughout, giving it a masculine feel.

She stops when she reaches a long marble bar bordering the kitchen. "Would you like something to drink?"

There's a glass of white wine sitting on the counter. "I'll have whatever you're having."

"Sancerre." She circles the bar and opens the refrigerator. "Is that okay?"

"Fine." I watch as she pours the glass, noticing her hand is trembling, a stab of guilt hitting me at how nervous I make her. She carries the beverage to me, grabbing hers as she passes.

"Summer." I wait until she meets my gaze. "We don't have to do this if you don't want to."

"I want to." She rushes out. "You just didn't text me back for so long. I didn't know if I did something wrong. I thought maybe you had changed your mind."

If she only knew what was going through my mind right now, she would run the other way. But of course, I don't tell her that. "I had work, other obligations."

She takes a long gulp of her wine. "Okay." Her eyes peek up at mine under her lashes. "So, we're good?"

"We're good." I walk to one of the couches. "But I would like to combine two of our lessons today. It will make things easier on my schedule." And my cock. And my sanity. And my conscious.

She sits a few feet away from me on the same couch, her face staining red as she asks her next question. "So, blow jobs and what then?"

"Has anyone ever licked your pussy, Summer?" My cock twitches at the mere thought, her open mouth calling like an invitation, providing the answer I was expecting.

Once she recovers from the shock of my question, she

stammers her response. "Wh-, Ho-, Why do you need to know that?"

"Because, little girl, you're going to want to know what it feels like when it's done well." I shift closer to her, my legs widening to accommodate the bulge growing between them. "But first, lesson number two." I take her free hand and place it over my cock. Her head snaps down to look at what she's holding, and then to my face.

"Take it out."

"How?" Her voice is barely a whisper.

"Kneel in front of me." I take her wine and place it on a nearby table. "Undo my belt, my pants, and pull down the zipper."

As her fingers start to work, the tip of her tongue sweeps across her lips, my cock stiffening further. When she completes her task, I decide to help, lifting my hips to shove my pants down off my waist, my cock springing free. She sits back on her heels, a small gasp escaping as her eyes lock onto my length.

"Have you done this before?" Part of me doesn't want to know. I want to believe my cock will be the first one between her perfect, cloud-like lips. The other part of me doesn't want her teeth raking down my skin, so I'm torn when she shakes her head.

She stays silent, her focus still between my thighs as I guide her hand to wrap around my cock. Her thumb slides across the tip, spreading the precum already leaking over the tip. Her attention finally diverts back to my eyes and she swallows loudly. "What should I do?"

"Show me what you would do." I cover her hand with

mine and squeeze, demonstrating how to hold me, then slide her hand up then down before letting go.

When she bends her head toward my cock, her eyes still on mine, I swear to God I almost come right then. She's so fucking perfect and she doesn't even know it. Her tongue slips out between her mouth and lands at the base of my cock then licks lazily up my length. I close my eyes, my head falling back against the couch. "That's perfect, Summer."

She trails her tongue up my shaft several more times until the heat of her mouth slides over the head, sucking just the crown inside. Holy Fuck. I don't need to teach her a damn thing. I thread my hand through her hair, gathering it in a loose bunch, then push her further down my length, almost exploding when she hums. My cock jerks inside her mouth, and I yank hard, pulling until she's looking up at me.

"Just where in the fuck did you learn to do that?" I hiss out.

"I did my homework." Her mouth twitches up at her reference to me telling her to watch porn during our last lesson. "Do I get a gold star?"

Jesus. Twelve days of porn and she's turned into a fucking minx. "Let's see if you can finish what you start, little girl." I jerk my chin toward my waist, another jolt shooting through me as she engulfs my dick in her heat again. This time, she needs no guidance from me. She bobs her head up and down my dick, sucking hard as she slides up, swirls her tongue around the tip then slides down again. I cradle her head in both my hands when she speeds up, her throat swallowing my cock when it hits the back of her throat.

I groan with each swallow, my fingers digging into her scalp, the pain seeming to edge her on, my hips thrusting into her mouth. My balls begin to tighten, signaling my impending release. "I'm going to come." I pant out, letting go of her head, wanting what happens next to be her choice. "You don't have to swallow." I insist, happy to finish with her fingers wrapped around me.

She waves me off, her grip locking around the bottom of my shaft, sucking me inside the fire of her mouth, her cheeks going hollow from the effort, and I explode. I let out a bellow, my cock pulsing my release down her throat, my hands clenching the material of the cushions into my palms as she swallows and swallows.

She draws slowly back, my limp cock falling from her mouth into my thatch of dark curls. She bites her lower lip between her teeth peeking up at me and I swear to fucking God, I feel like I'm in heaven. She looks like a damn angel.

"Still think I'm a little girl?" She places her hands on my knees, pushing against them to stand up. Her nipples are hard, the peaks rising through the thin material of her top. No, I don't think she's a little girl at all anymore. Not at fucking all.

Chapter Six

~Summer~

He grabs his wine off the table and chugs it in two large gulps, setting the empty glass where it was. He turns his eyes to me, his voice gravelly when he speaks. "Your turn."

I take a step back, the smug contentment I was just boasting swept away by those two small words. "Don't you need to rest for a few minutes?"

He rises, tucking himself back into his jeans, fastening the button, then the buckle, his dark irises never leaving me. "Scared, little girl?" He takes another step, closing the distance between us, his fingers stroking down my cheek. "We can stop anytime you'd like."

"Stop saying that." Anger boiling up from my belly as

I shove his hand away. "You know that's not what I want."

"Just making sure." He doesn't move, still crowding me as he lowers his gaze down my body and then back up. "The dress would have been better today."

"I can't seem to win with you." My eyes narrow as I glare at him. "I didn't bring a change of clothes with me, so you're going to have to deal with this."

"Get undressed."

"I'm sorry, what?"

His fingers move to my pants and start working the button. "I can't very well eat you out with your clothes on." Before I can object, his fingers slide into the waistband pushing them down my legs, the material dropping to the floor. He takes my hand and walks backward. "Step out."

I comply because objecting at this point would seem silly, and also, not what I want. I stop when he does, my heart galloping in my chest. The grip he has on my hand releases to trail up the length of my arm, the hairs rising in the wake of his touch. He skims all the way up under my chin, lifting it until I'm looking up at him.

"Are you scared?"

It's the first considerate thing he's asked me since he's arrived. I blink, my eyes scanning the angle of his chin, his sculpted cheekbones, his red lips, parted slightly as he waits for me to reply. I finally lift my eyes to his and shake my head. "I want to kiss you."

His eyes close for several seconds, his nostrils flaring before they reopen. "Next time."

"But-" I press my body flush to his as I protest, stopping when I feel his fingers lift the hem of my shirt, peeling it off my body, separating us a few inches.

He leans toward me, the heat of his breath against my ear when he speaks. "Lesson three is about foreplay." His hands grip my waist to turn my body as he walks me backward, stopping when my legs hit the couch. "I'm going to show you how a man should make you feel. To make sure you're ready for him. To make sure the experience isn't just about him." His lips trail against the rim of my ear, his tongue skimming the lobe, a small sigh slipping from me. "To make you feel like nothing else in the world exists except you."

"Okay." I murmur, my head rolling back as he drags his tongue down my throat, his arms wrapping around my back as he lowers me onto the couch. He removes my bra in one swift motion, my legs parting as he positions himself over me. I feel the heat of his mouth on my nipple a second before his tongue laves over the peak, my back arching into him.

"Does that feel good, little one?" He drags his tongue over my other nipple, this time closing his mouth around it before flicking the hard bud with the tip of his tongue.

I mewl out a response which I think resembles a yes, my fingers weaving into his soft locks as I press him into my chest.

"I know, I know." He coos as he alternates between nipping then sucking each of my breasts, my core throbbing between my legs. I try to ease the ache by pushing myself against his thigh, groaning in frustration when he grips a hand around my waist to hold it down.

"Don't worry, I'm going to take care of that for you." He assures me, his hand gliding lower to cup my center with his palm. His fingers continue rubbing in a circular motion as he sucks a raised peak between his lips, his teeth latching onto the tip, biting it, a gush of heat flaring between my legs. I groan, my fingernails clawing into his shirt as I try to get enough traction to shove my center forcefully into his hand.

He chuckles, the vibration from his chest an inch from mine. "You want more my little vixen?"

"Yes." I drag my hands down to the hem of his shirt to try to lift it. "Take this off." He lifts his mouth off my breast to look at me. "Please." He stares at me a second, but then rises to his knees, yanking the shirt over his head before dropping it to the floor.

Holy Hell. His body is like a chiseled masterpiece. It literally looks like one of the statues I've seen at the museum. The gorgeous white ones that resemble the gods. I loop a finger into the waist of his pants to tug him closer. I feather my fingers over his torso feeling every bump and ridge, the urge to kiss him growing as I trail lower. I lick my lips, peering up at his and surge forward until I feel his mouth against mine. He lets me kiss him, but only for a second before he tears his mouth away, his eyes flashing to mine.

Before I can say a word, he slides down my body, his hands gripping the seam of my panties as he does, peeling them off me. Without warning, his head is between my legs, his tongue dragging in one long swipe over my slit. My hands fling to his head, my fingers clutching onto his hair when he blows a hot breath over the streak he just trailed, then he licks me again.

"Oh my God." I drawl out, realizing this is so much better than my fingers. His tongue dives deeper between my folds finding my clit. He flicks it back and forth, blowing on it, my back rising off the couch when he slides a finger inside and begins pumping it in and out. His tongue moves faster, harder over my clit, my head thrashing back and forth as I feel my body react, my muscles starting to tighten. Xander slides a second finger inside and thrusts deeper, his tongue never slowing as I feel my hips raise of the couch.

"Xander." I chant as every molecule centers at the apex of my body, detonating when he draws my clit between his lips and sucks. I hear a scream that I recognize as my own, and then break into a thousand tiny pieces that scatter across the universe, igniting into sparks of dust as I come back to earth. I can't open my eyes, even when I feel him rise off my body, soft spasms still shudder through me. Panted breaths puff from between my lips as muscles relax one by one, and still, I can't lift my lids. I hear Xander moving around me, sighing when he drapes something soft over my body, but I'm still reeling from the sensations I just experienced and feel paralyzed.

It's not until I hear the elevator doors slide shut with a bang that I'm ripped back to reality and bolt upright. I listen for a moment then call out. "Xander?" I stand, wrapping a blanket around my body and walk down the hall and call his name again. As I reach the elevator, I can hear it descending and realize he left. Just like that. He left.

Chapter Seven

~Xander~

I glower at her text for the tenth time. She sent it yesterday, just a few minutes after I left, and like the bastard I am, I haven't responded. It's a simple question. "Where did you go?" Unfortunately, it doesn't have a simple answer.

The more time I spend with her, the deeper I can feel her digging into me. With her innocence, her beauty, her trust; stirring something inside of me. My heart, which I thought had turned cold and dark long ago, seems to flicker to life whenever I'm around her. I had to leave before she opened her eyes because I knew, without a doubt, if she had asked me to stay, I would have. And that would not only be bad for her, it would be bad for me.

She has no idea what kind of appetite I have, the damage I could do to her, and I won't do that to her. I sit for a long time pondering my next move, surprising even myself when I grab my phone and call her. She picks up on the second ring.

"Hello?"

"Hi." I wait to see if she's going to say anything, but when she doesn't, I start. "I'm sorry about leaving."

"Is that what I should expect from someone?" She whispers.

"No. Never." I rake a hand through my unruly locks. "Generally, my customers, my clients, prefer it when I disappear after. Having me around is a reminder of whatever sin they've just committed." I blow out a breath. "I forgot that you weren't like my regular clients though. You're in a box all your own."

"Oh." She's quiet a moment, then speaks. "Now what?"

I wish I fucking knew. If I admit to myself what I want to come next, I'd probably scare the hell out of both of us. Instead, I tell her what I've decided. "We're going on a date."

"A date?" She echoes.

"Yep." I confirm. "Our fourth lesson is supposed to be about intimacy. Being intimate means getting to know each other. Learning things about each other that either leads to attraction and takes you to that next level, or sends you running in the opposite direction."

"Okay." She states. "And then what?"

"And then, you'll have the tools you need to decide. Is he worthy of you? Your time, your mind, your lips, and eventually, your body. I think by now, you know what to do from there."

"Yes, I think you've covered that quite well." She admits.

"Be ready at seven p.m. on Friday. I'll pick you up." I instruct. "Wear something nice. Something you would wear if it was a real date."

"It's not?"

I take pause at her question, then answer. "It will be our last lesson."

"But you said five." She reminds me.

"You'll be fine. More than fine." And a fifth lesson would take me to a place I'm not ready to go. I need to let her go sooner than later, before my feelings swallow me whole.

"If you say so." She relents. "I'll be in my new apartment then. My student housing was available early."

"Do you have the address?"

"556 West 113th Street. Room 3F."

"You're going to Columbia?" My interest piquing as I glance over at the pile of mail on my desk, my class schedules in the mix.

"Yes, how did you know?" Curiosity in her voice.

"That's just several blocks from me. I familiar with the area." I explain, hoping she doesn't press any further. "I'll see you Friday, then."

"At seven." She confirms.

I hang up without warning and can imagine her staring at the phone, marveling again at my callousness.

At exactly seven o'clock Friday, I step out of the car I

hired and approach the entrance for the address she provided. I'd never actually been inside any of the student housing, even though I had lived in my current location for the last five years. I didn't tend to mingle with any of the students at the college given my preference for paying customers at Temptations. I walk through the doors and locate an elevator, taking it up to the third floor. I find her room easily enough and knock.

A minute later the door swings open, a sharp inhale catching my breath when she steps into sight. "You look stunning."

She's wearing a silky black dress, with flowing ruffles on both sides of a V-neck keyhole, that travels down until they meet in the middle, continuing until the hem. The waist is fitted but then loose once past the hips, flaring out just slightly mid-thigh, showcasing her long, lean legs. The strappy heels she's wearing are a perfect match to the silver chain weaved into the collar tying the dress at the back of her neck. Her hair is loose, flowing over her shoulders in soft waves. Crisp, blue eyes stare back at me, her lips tinted a light pink, almost the same color as her flushed cheeks.

"Thank you." She takes a step back. "Would you like to come in? It's a little messy. I'm still trying to get organized."

"I have a car waiting. We should probably leave now if we want to make our reservation. It's for seven-thirty and there's traffic."

"Okay." She twists around to snatch a set of keys and a

small clutch off a bookcase, then turns back to me. "Let's go."

She locks the door, slipping the keys into the bag when she's done, and we stroll to the elevator. The door opens immediately when I press the call button, so we step inside. As soon as we're in the enclosed space I smell her. I'm not certain if it's her perfume, her shampoo, or lotion, but it surrounds me in a light powdery, floral scent that has me taking an unconscious step closer as I drag a deep breath in.

She turns her head, her eyes widening when she notices. "Are you okay?"

The elevator dings, announcing our arrival to the lobby, her attention diverted long enough for me to avoid the question. I place my hand on the small of her back to urge her forward. "The car's right out front."

Once we're seated, I give the driver the address of the restaurant and we're off.

"Where are we going?" Her feet are crossed at the ankles, her legs tucked to the side, her hands folded in her lap.

"A place called RH Rooftop." If I thought being in the elevator with her was difficult, this was torture. I clear my throat. "Have you been before?"

She shakes her head. "I really haven't been anywhere in the city yet. A few places out at the Hamptons."

"You'll like it." Without thought, I take her hand and slide it between mine, resting it on my thigh. Her eyes follow the movements, but she doesn't say a thing. "It's a beautiful night to eat outside under the stars."

One side of her mouth tilts down. "Why are you being so nice? You're never nice."

A small chuff of laughter bubbles up. "It's a date."

"I thought it was a lesson." She counters, angling her head.

"Touché." I chuckle again.

"Is this how things work when you're escorting? If the price is right, you paint on a smile, splash on some amazing smelling cologne, dress nicely and behave?"

"Someone's a little angry this evening?" I purse my lips, one brow arching high.

"You said five lessons." She shifts, facing me. "You combine two lessons into one, and then said I didn't need the fifth, so now we're down to three. Three lessons for ten thousand dollars. I'm just not sure that's fair. And I'm thinking that I should get a little more for my money."

Her knee is bouncing up and down in time to the short breaths leaving her. I lift one of my hands off hers and place it over her bare leg, applying light pressure to stop her nervous movement. She glances at my hand before snapping her eyes to mine.

"You don't think you're getting your money's worth?" I lean closer, lowering my voice as I drag my hand up between her legs, stopping when I reach the hem of her dress. "Do you want me to touch you right now? You're probably already wet. I bet I could make you come in less than a minute."

Her eyes dart to the front of the car toward the driver, then back to me.

"You think he hasn't seen or heard worse in the back of this car?" I continue to taunt her.

"I'd rather you take me home and make love to me." She whispers back, my cock jerking against my zipper at her suggestion.

"It's called fucking, Summer." I sit back, sliding my hand off her leg. "And that wasn't part of the deal."

"Neither was three lessons. It was five." She crosses her arms over her chest. "That would be two thousand a lesson. So, I figure I have a four-thousand-dollar credit right now." She tilts closer, hissing the next words. "I would think that would cover *fucking* me."

"You don't want me." My jaw tightening as I clench my fingers into a tight ball. "Wait for someone that is special to you. Someone that will make you the center of his universe and treat you like the princess you deserve to be treated. You shouldn't have to pay anyone to have sex with you. You're better than a one-night stand and that's all I can be to you."

"You don't know anything about what I want." She murmurs under her breath, turning to look out the window.

"I would like for us to have a nice time tonight, even without the fucking." I place a finger under her chin to turn her face to mine. "If you think you can stop pouting long enough."

"I'm not pouting." Her plump bottom lip jutting out. Unable to help myself, I tilt forward, swipe my tongue over the tender flesh and kiss her. Her breath is warm and tastes like apples. I don't linger, just giving her enough to hopefully stop her overthinking us sleeping together.

I pull back, one corner of my mouth crooking up at how her eyes are still closed. "Open your eyes, Summer." I skim my fingers down her cheek, her lids blinking open. "We're here."

Less than ten minutes later we're seated in a beautiful corner booth, small lush trees on either side of us, a shimmering crystal chandelier centered above our round table. "This is so pretty."

"I knew you would like it." I smile across the table. "It's simple elegance at its best. Very much like you."

Her cheeks blush as she looks down at the menu. "What do you recommend?"

"The salmon is really good, or if you're a steak person, the rib eye is amazing."

"Let's get each of those and we can share?" She suggests, biting her lip, looking across at me.

"That's a great idea." I slide the menu from her fingers. "Trust me with the wine?"

She nods, her lips curving into a smile. "I think it's safe to say I trust you, considering what I've let you do to me."

Before I can respond, our server appears. I order a bottle of Silver Oak Cabernet, Gem lettuce salads to start, and the salmon and steak, medium, in case she doesn't like it too rare. Once he's gone, I direct my attention back to her. "So, you're going to Columbia?"

"Yes." She takes a sip of water. "For the next few years anyway. I just finished my Bachelor's in Business at the

University of Vermont, but I think I want to get my Master's in Environmental Sciences."

"You *think* you want to get your Master's?" I press for more information.

She purses her lips a moment before answering. "Can I be honest?"

"Please." I nod my head indicating she should continue.

"I just wasn't sure what I wanted to do with myself yet." She frowns as she continues. "I think I want to go work for my family's company, but not yet. I feel like I haven't even lived yet, and to box myself into a career I'll probably be at forever." She shrugs. "I figured, come to New York, see what it's like. See what *I* like."

"I think that's smart." The waiter appears with our wine, opens it, pouring us each a glass after I give my approval.

"I mean, Columbia will be good for me. It's important for me to understand how I might be able to improve how my family's business can provide energy in a way that's better for our environment. There's too much at stake for future generations if we continue to consume energy the way we do now."

I'm impressed. She didn't just want to live off her family's money. She wanted to learn and work and make a difference in the world. It was a rare thing to find among the many rich women I'd encountered.

"What about you Xander? Are you just going to be a giga-I mean, an escort for the rest of your life?" She takes a large sip of wine. "How does one even get into that line of work?"

"Oh, Summer, you don't ever hold back what you're thinking, do you?" Sipping from my glass, I look over the rim debating if I want to share what I do with her.

I could tell her that I'm a professor at the very college she'll be attending in a few weeks, but I don't know if I want to open that door. Columbia is a big campus with many buildings and classrooms. The chances are slim that we would even encounter each other, but still.

"I'm sorry. I know that was rude." She fidgets with the silverware next to her plate. "I guess I'm trying to rationalize why you have sex for a living."

"Maybe because I love fucking. And it's less complicating then dating and all the expectations that go into that." The waiter appears as I'm speaking, his face turning crimson as he places our salads in front of us and quickly disappears.

She remains silent so I continue. "I started working for Temptations during my last year of school. A friend told me about them and I applied. I was good looking and I knew how to use my manners. It was an easy job that paid exceptionally well."

"And you just never stopped?" She takes a bite of her salad.

"At first, I never slept with my clients. I initially did it for the company. I liked being around women, but loved that there were no strings attached even more. And then one time, when a date I was attracted to asked, I said yes.

She paid me two grand to spend a few hours with her. Needless to say, after that, I rarely said no."

"It sounds dirty." She judges, her nose scrunching.

"You have to understand, these women, and sometimes men, are beautiful and intriguing. Not dirty, although sometimes the sex was. And I always wear a condom. Always."

"And you like it?"

"Most of the time." I drag a hand down my face, then meet her in the eye, revealing more than I probably should. "I don't have to say yes. I can say no. And I do, more often than not these days. As priorities in my life have changed, so have my reasons for doing this."

"Like you're saying no to me." Her voice firm but soft.

Timing could not be better when the server shows up with our entrees, allowing me to escape responding. We split our meals, sharing with each other, the conversation turning to safer topics about the food and the restaurant.

We finish the bottle of wine, her cheeks rosier for it, and her overall demeanor much more relaxed. I pay the bill and call for the driver. We board the elevator, my hand staying on her lower back after I guide her in. She leans into me, her body warm, my hand wrapping around her waist to hold her closer. She peers up at me, her irises so blue in contrast to her long, dark lashes.

"What is it?" I ask, curious what she's thinking.

"Didn't you say there would be kissing?"

Chapter Eight

A wide grin spreads across his face, dimples imploding in his cheeks, and I swear to God, my panties feel like they might combust from the heat that just sparked between my legs. "Patience, little girl."

"Ugh." I pull away, immediately missing the heat of his body. "I hate when you call me that." The doors to the elevator slide open and I stride through, my heels clicking angrily against the marble floor. I hear him call my name, but I don't stop.

His fingers wrap around my wrist, and before I can blink, he spins me around, and crushes his lips to mine. I gasp in surprise, my knees almost giving out when his tongue brushes against mine, then dips inside to tangle with it. He tastes like butter and wine and he's so very warm as he pulls me flush. My arms weave around his neck to hold on, gravity seeming to no longer be a factor in my world.

After a few minutes, or maybe just a few seconds, I honestly don't know, he pulls away, dropping one last soft kiss to my mouth as he does. I stare at him, my chest rising and falling with quick breaths.

"Will that do for now?" His voice sexy and low, one side of his mouth rising in a cocky grin.

"I'm just wondering what the lesson is here?" My hands still wrapped around his neck.

He laughs out loud, his chest vibrating against mine, his eyes bright. "Has anyone ever kissed you like that?"

I think about the boys, and yes, I think they must all be considered boys after the few short encounters I've had with Xander, and realize that not a single one ever left a fire burning in my belly the way it was now. My muscles tremble as I blink up at him, then shake my head once to indicate my response.

"Then you just learned what a good kiss should feel like." He states, smugness in his tone as he straightens to his full height, one hand staying firmly on my waist. "Come on, the car will be waiting."

I let him lead me, my mind too busy wondering if there will be more kissing or if that was to be my only lesson. I can't deny that I want more, so much more than just that one kiss, as I slide into the leather seat of the car. When Xander's settled, he gives the driver my address, his hand resting on my thigh, his thumb rubbing small circles against my skin. There is a naughty part of me that wants to spread my legs wide and push his hand higher, but I'm too afraid he'll laugh, or worse, push me away. Instead, I swing my face to his and ask him a question I think takes him by surprise. "Tell me how a man likes to be kissed?"

"What?" His eyes widening.

"How do I know when I should kiss a man? And how should I kiss him? Should I pepper small kisses over his lips, or should I tease him with my tongue before I slip it into his mouth?"

"Just how much porn have you been watching, little girl?" His question is practically a growl.

"Enough to know that I'm not sure. There's not a lot of kissing in those videos." I muse.

He chuffs back a laugh, then wraps an arm around me to haul me to him. "Kiss me." He invites, my pulse beating in my ears. "I'm telling you to. That's how you know when a man wants you to kiss him."

I lick my lips, my gaze sliding from his eyes to his mouth. I'm not exactly sure what to do, so I let my body take over and act on instinct. I tilt my head and with the tip of my tongue, swipe it across his bottom lip. His mouth parts and I propel myself against his chest as I seal my lips to his. My hand snakes up to grip onto the hair at the scruff of his neck and I tug, sliding my tongue against his when his mouth opens wider. He shifts my body so that I'm sitting across his lap, his arousal pressing into my thigh, my other hand moving to clench the material of his shirt in my fist.

I drag my mouth off his to leave a trail of kisses across his cheek until I reach his ear. I sweep my tongue around his lobe, and then nibble, my breath hot as I feel it blow into his ear. He groans, and it feels powerful, knowing my kiss is making him feel this way. To have him react to me this way. My lips curve up in a small smile of triumph as I whisper in his ear. "Is that how little girls kiss?"

His hand latches onto my hair, yanking me back so my face is even with his, a wicked gleam in his eyes. "That's the kind of kiss that will get you in trouble."

"I think we both know the trouble I want to get into with you."

His eyes lock onto mine, staring into them for several long seconds before he slides me off his lap. "Summer, don't push this. Not now when all I want to do is lift your skirt, bend you over this seat and fuck you."

"I'm asking you to fuck me." I remind him. I turn my body to his and plead my case again. "Xander, you tell me that when I have sex with someone it should be special, and with someone I care about. Someone who will know what I want and make sure the experience is something I'll treasure and remember fondly."

"I know what I said, and I mean it." He confirms.

"You are that person for me." I clutch his hand between mine and press it to my chest. "I've shared more about myself with you than anyone. I care about you, and know being with you would be special and something I will always remember and cherish. To know and understand what it should feel like to be made love to." He rolls his eyes, so I correct myself. "Okay, to be fucked properly."

The car stops and the driver turns as he opens the door. "I'll wait outside, sir." Holy shit, I just shared all that with the driver too. I was so caught up in the moment that I didn't even realize. I feel my face flame as I peek back at Xander to find him looking intently at me.

"Let me walk you up to your room. It's dark now." Disappointment floods through me as he steps out of the car and moves around to my side to help me out. I take his hand, his hold tightening when I'm out the car, keeping me close. He pauses and speaks to the driver. "You don't have to wait." Hope blooms in my chest, until I hear what he says next. "I live a couple of blocks away and want to walk home."

Dreading what happens next, I attempt to end things here on the sidewalk instead of in a hallway upstairs. "I'm fine from here. You don't have to escort me." The double meaning of my words purely accidental, but no less true.

"No." He tugs my hand and starts toward the doors of the building, making it clear he isn't going to change his mind. "I'll see you in."

We take the elevator to the third floor, my fingers still entwined with his in a vise like hold, as we exit and walk in silence down the hall, stopping when we reach my room. I try to slide my hand out of his so I can grab my keys from my clutch, but his grip tightens as he lifts it above my head and pushes my back up against the door. He steps into my space, tilting into me, his normally light eyes, dark as he peers down. "I want to take you inside this room and do everything you want me to, but I'm afraid it's going to mean more to you than it should."

"So what if it does." I blink, my heart racing inside my chest. I lick my lips, dry from the short breaths racing in and out of me. "Something like this should be special to me, but I'm not foolish enough to confuse it for anything other than what it is for you."

"And just what do you think this is?" His mouth just an inch from mine, his eyes darting back and forth.

"Your job." I breathe out softly.

"This stopped being a job the minute I let you kiss me." And then, his lips press against mine in a kiss so searing I feel the heat of it all the way to my toes. Somehow, he manages to get the keys from my purse and into the lock of the door without breaking his hold on me. I almost fall backwards when the door flies open, but he drops the keys and bag to the floor, sliding his hands around my waist to clasp me close. He urges me further into the room, kicking the door closed with his foot, the sound of it slamming loud in the quiet of my room.

I want to slow this down but I'm afraid if I do, he'll change his mind, so I seize onto his shoulders, clinging to his body like a life preserver. I can feel his hard length against my stomach, a groan sounding between us when I grind into it. He pushes me back, my hold on him lost as he takes two steps away, separating us.

"Wait." My heart stops, my breath caught in my throat as I assume what's coming next. "We shouldn't rush this."

My heart skipping back to life when his words register. "Okay."

"Come here." He beckons me with a tilt of his chin. I obey, closing the distance in two strides. He cradles my face with his palms, lifting it, his lips feathering over my cheeks, my eyes, the tip of my nose until they brush delicately over mine. A small gasp puffs from me when his fingers flutter over one erect nipple before trailing lower, sliding under the hem of my dress. They skim higher, along the back of my thigh until his entire hand cups my ass, squeezing tenderly. His other hand moves to the back of my neck to tug at the tie holding my dress up, releasing it, the silk material sliding down to my waist.

He backs away, his gaze travelling down my torso and then back to my face. "Take it off."

I comply, no hesitation. He's seen me before, and I've never been shy about being naked. I shove the dress over my hips letting it fall to the floor, stepping out of it, my body now clad in just a strapless bra and thong. Yes, I broke a thong out for this date.

"You are simply exquisite." He steps close enough to drift a soft touch up the length of my arm, over my shoulder and around the back of my neck, tilting it to stroke his tongue over my lips before sweeping a gentle kiss across my mouth. I sigh, pleasure coursing through me from his slightest touch.

I want to feel him as well, so as he continues to caress my mouth, I reach for the buttons of his shirt to work them open. When my task is complete, I thread between the breach in the material and spread the cotton, placing my hands flat on his chest. One hand rests over his heart and I can feel it's quick pace and marvel at its speed. He's as excited as me. He's not pretending or acting and it spurs me to act more boldly, my hands grazing over the bumps of his abdomen until they reach his buckle.

His hot mouth rakes down the side of my neck, nipping and sucking at my skin, the ache between my legs throbbing. As I unfasten his belt and begin to unclasp his pants, his hands snake behind my back and release my bra, my breasts exposed as it falls to the floor. He toes his shoes off then moves his hands to his pants, pushing them and his briefs off in one shove. He shrugs his shirt off, and in the blink of an eye he stands before me naked.

He moves to kiss me, his hand reaching for my face, but I place mine flat on his chest, stopping him. With a small shake of my head and a look that I hope tells him what he needs to know, I place my other hand against the hard plain of his torso, and begin exploring each inch of his body. His skin is soft, but his muscles a contradiction under my fingertips, and when I drag on digit over his nipple, he hisses as his cock jerks in response. "Careful, little girl."

It's a warning I don't heed, inclining forward to lave my tongue over the raised peak, my hand grazing lower to curl around his hard length, his fingers tangling through my locks on a groan. I drag another wet lick over the nipple then creep lower until I reach his belly button. I swirl around the small circle then flick my tongue inside, cum leaking from the tip of his length. My eyes dart up, meeting his, locking my gaze, as I kneel lower to swipe the liquid dripping from him. It's salty and a little bitter, but when his mouth falls open with a long sigh, I want to give him more.

I slide him between my lips and inhale, sucking his length deep into my throat, his nails digging into my scalp when I swallow. His knees buckle slightly when I slide back then bob my head back down in one quick motion, taking him even deeper. I feel heat pool in my center as it spasms, aching for him to be inside me. I hum in pleasure, the only way I can express how good this feels, then feel myself being pulled up as he yanks me off his cock with a pop to slam his mouth to mine.

He rips away, panting, his eyes darting wildly to mine, one brow arching. "You're too fucking good at that, and when I come, it's going to be inside you."

"Oh." Can't argue with that, but somehow, I seemed to have lost any ability to communicate.

He presses a kiss to my lips then leads me to my bed. "Lay down." As I comply, he walks quickly to his pants, pulling out his wallet and then a condom. It hits me then that this is really and truly happening. He's not going to leave. He's going to have sex with me. The first real sex I've ever had. Instead of being nervous or scared, my body relaxes, a state of joy washing over me at having him to share this moment with.

When he reaches me, he bends over me with a hand on either side of my shoulders, lowering his face to brush a kiss against my mouth. He inches lower, nuzzling down my neck, weaving a hot path to my breast, drawing it between his lips on a soft pull. My back arches as I gasp, my arms lashing out beside me as my hands clench onto the comforter, the material bunching into tight balls between my fingers.

His other hand snakes over the scrap of material covering my center, and begins to glide back and forth against my swollen lips, my thighs spreading. I clench my lids closed, the myriad of sensation swirling through me almost too much to process. A finger slides under the silk and flicks my clit, my eyes popping open as I let out a loud groan, the ache between my legs intensifying as I crave something more. As if he can read my mind, he glides two digits through my slick center then sinks them inside of me.

"Oh, God." I sigh, thrusting my hips into his hand, still wanting more.

"You're so wet." He murmurs above me. "Just need to taste you."

His words send a bolt of lightning straight to my core, the anticipation of his tongue spurring my desire for him even higher. His fingers slide out of me to peel my thong off. He settles between my legs, his hands spreading me wider. He leans in and inhales deeply. "Jesus you even smell fucking amazing." And then, he flattens his tongue against the very bottom of my ass and drags it all the way up until it licks against my clit.

Every muscle in my body contracts, and I let out a groan that I swear comes from the very bottom of my soul. He chuckles, the vibration transferring onto my clit as he strokes over me again, and without warning I explode. Yelling out my surprise, my pussy pulsates wildly around his mouth as he sucks, my hips pushed into the mattress as he grips them to hold me in place. I call out to God repeatedly, I think thanking the heavens for the bliss I'm feeling, only stopping when Xander drags his mouth off my center to slide up my body to swallow them down.

His lips are slick and covered in my juices, but I don't care. I just want more. A yearning I didn't know could exist, creating a hunger in me that felt like starvation. "Please Xander." I mewl into his mouth, arching my body into his as I beg for him to quench this new feeling. "Please."

He rolls off me, grabbing the condom off the bed, ripping it open. Rolling the smooth rubber over his shaft, he locks his gaze onto mine. "Are you ready?" His question his gentle, his tone caring, and I nod, never being more sure of anything in my life. "I'm going to go slow. Tell me if it's too much."

I'm not a virgin, but this will also be the first time that a man, a real man, will be entering me and I'm quite sure, staying in me for more than a minute. The fact that he's acknowledging this, taking every precaution to make this moment beautiful and special, warms me. I nod, and go to speak, but he covers my mouth with his, kissing me with a tenderness I didn't know he possessed.

I sigh into his mouth, my arms wrapping around his body to hold him as he uses one hand to guide himself to my center. He pushes in just a little, his lips moving to my ear and begins whispering to me. "You're so beautiful." Another small thrust deeper, my mouth forming a small O as my core clenches. "Fucking perfect." Another thrust, this time even deeper, a moan rolling from me. "So fucking tight." One final shove and he's all the way in, my nails dragging across his back when he slides back and then plunges all the way into me again, both of us moaning.

"Are you okay?" His breath hot against my ear, his fingers brushing across my cheek before he plants small kisses to my lips.

"Yes." I breath against his mouth. "Please don't stop."

"No." He pumps in and out of me. "I won't." His mouth covering mine again, devouring every breath I pant as he continues to thrust, his hips rocking faster, harder until I feel myself start to climb. I curl into him, my hands scraping the skin on his back as I try to get closer, and he shifts his hips, his length grinding over my clit and I scream, another orgasm exploding from me. Xander's hips pound into me a final time, my name roaring from him as I feel his cock pulsing between my clenched walls, each of us clinging to the other as we float weightless.

I drift back to consciousness when I feel him slide out of me, his lips feathering over my mouth as he speaks. "I'll be right back." And he is. A moment later his arms wrap around me, pulling me against his warmth, kisses pressing onto the top of my head as he cradles me. "Are you okay?"

"Uh-huh." I hum out, snuggling my body further into his, entwining my fingers into one of his. "Thank you,

Alexander." It's the first time I've ever called him by his full name, but this meant so much to me. It didn't matter that I paid him. Nothing could have ever been more special to me than what he just did and shared with me.

"You're welcome, Summer." He uses my name as well, and not Little Girl. His fingers squeeze mine gently, and bathed in his warmth, I fall asleep.

I wake many hours later, surprised when I see the sun shining through the one window in my room, but not surprised that Xander is gone. Other than covering me with a blanket, and the slight ache between my legs, there is no evidence that he was ever here.

I rise, stretch, then slide off the bed. I pause when I notice something on the bookcase next to the door. I pad over, lifting it, my heart stilling when I realize it's the same envelope I gave to Xander containing the money. I turn it over, my breath catching when I start to read the words he wrote.

Summer,

Being with you was an honor, never a job, and taking money would be wrong. I'll cherish every moment as dearly as you deserve to be. Farewell my little one.

XO Alexander

I read the words over and over again, my fingers trembling around the envelope as I digest his message. He took something that could have been perceived as dirty, and made it clean with this one action. He showed me he cared, and I mattered, and that what we did mattered. I press the envelope to my heart, then hide it between two books in the case. I smile, grateful and at peace, knowing I made the right choice in him. Yes, it was over, but I felt like I had just begun and couldn't wait for the next chapter of my life to begin.

Chapter Nine

~Summer~

It's my second day of classes at Columbia, and so far, things have been great. Of course, yesterday's class was a course on climatology that I found utterly fascinating.

Today's class, Advanced Physics, not so much. Math was a subject I could take or leave, and something I always struggled with. I technically should have taken it while I was at the University of Vermont, but didn't.

It was a required course in the curriculum in order to earn my Master's, so here I was, dragging my feet as I made my way into the math building.

I pulled out my phone to confirm the room number as I entered the building:

Advanced Physics
Professor A. Walker
Math Building, Room 108

At least it was on the first floor. Most of these older buildings didn't have elevators, and lugging a backpack loaded with a laptop and heavy text books up several flights of stairs was not exactly the kind of work out I favored. I find the door labeled 108 and enter, surprised to see the room is already more than half full. I try to always be early, never wanting to be the student that bursts in late, forever marking herself with a great, big, giant X with the instructor. No thanks.

We'll be doing labs in this class, so there are rows of tables, with two stools per table, set up throughout the room. There are only a few tables in the front of the room still available, so I weave through the rows and stop at a table where one stool appears to be free.

"Is this seat taken?" I ask the person at the table. His head is down, his hair a bit longer, shielding his face.

When he turns and lifts a smile in my direction, I practically swoon at how handsome he is. "It's all yours." He nods toward the stool.

"Thanks." I fumble nervously trying to step up onto the seat, his eyes watching my every move as I finally get my footing and sit down, swinging my backpack onto the table.

"I'm Blake Davenport." He stretches a hand out in

front of me, a dimple appearing in his right cheek as his smile deepens.

Of course, his name is Blake Davenport. His middle name is probably James or Jeffries. He had that, *I just got off a sailboat in Newport, Rhode Island*, look about him. Sandy blonde hair, tan, dimples, strong chin. Trouble, that's what he was going to be. I slide my hand into his, returning his smile. "Summer Knight. Nice to meet you."

"I hope you're the smart one, otherwise these labs are going to kick our asses." He chuckles, folding his arms on the table as he leans toward me.

"I was hoping you were the smart one." I jest back.

"Well, I guess that means we'll just have to spend that much more time together studying."

He winks playfully, his comment laced with an underlying suggestion, which of course causes my cheeks to heat. Before I have a chance to respond, a commanding voice drags my attention to the front of the room. My heart plunges to my stomach in recognition, my mouth falling open as I'm unable to hide my surprise as cool, dark eyes lock onto mine.

"Good morning class." The entire room grows silent as he continues, his eyes finally leaving mine to scan the room. "I'm Professor Alexander Walker, your instructor for this course."

Holy shit! Xander, my Xander, is a fucking professor at Columbia! That's his day job? There is absolutely no way I can be stuck in a classroom with him for the next four months.

I close my gapping mouth, my knuckles turning white as I grip the pencil in my fingers, my eyes widening as his meet mine again. "I'm so looking forward to teaching you more over the next few months."

An almost imperceptible smirk plays across his lips as he continues, his words conveying so much more than others can be aware, as he turns and begins writing on the white board. So much for that new chapter I thought I was starting.

Chapter Ten

I knew I shouldn't be taking any pleasure in the shocked expression she's wearing. Even worse, I hate that my heart stutters upon seeing her again. I had missed her. It had been three long weeks of torture. I remembered every touch, every kiss, every moan that tumbled from her puffy lips. I craved more. And it took every ounce of my self control not to call her, not to run back to her dorm, not to take her again during these last three weeks. But, once I got my student roster and saw her name, another line had been drawn that I knew couldn't be crossed. This was going to be the longest damn semester of my life.

I try like hell, but can't seem to stop shifting my gaze in her direction every thirty seconds. She no longer looks like she's seen a ghost, but it's clear, from the glint shining through her narrowed eyes, she's not happy to see me. And who the hell is that sitting next to her? They seemed to be pretty chummy, sharing cheeky grins, completely oblivious to my arrival when I strolled into the room. Watching her expression change from one of joy to pure shock was the only thing that tampered the flash of heat burning in my gut.

Somehow, I manage to get through the class agenda, nearly shouting in relief when I dismiss the class. My consolation is short lived however when Summer heads in my direction instead of the exit.

"Xander," she starts, my hand raising, my palm and fingers flat, indicating she should stop.

"You mean, Professor Walker." I arch a brow, with a tilt of my head, hoping she understands my silent reprisal. "Perhaps we should take this discussion to my office, Ms. Knight?"

Her lips purse in a thin line, but she nods her agreement, following as I lead her to a door at the back of the class, and into a hallway. We're both silent, our footsteps echoing against the narrow walls as we walk. I stop when I reach my door, pull the key from my pocket, turn it in the lock, then push it open. I move inside, pressing myself flush against the wood, motioning for her to come in. She breezes past me, her fingers clutching her book bag at her side, her scent wafting over me. I close my eyes and inhale, absorbing every molecule of her light, floral aroma floating in the air around me. My dick twitches at the memory her smell evokes, my lids flying open as I turn to adjust myself while shutting the door firmly.

When I spin around, I find myself mere inches from her, halting me in my tracks, a frown tugging my mouth down. I step to her left, moving behind the safety of my desk, and sit down. She twists her body, her eyes tracking my every move, but she stays in place.

"Summer, please, take a seat." I point to one of the chairs on the other side of my desk.

Her face scrunches up as she continues to analyze me, but she does as requested, and slides into the chair closest to her, shifting her book bag to her lap.

"You're a professor?" The question falling from her full, pouty lips laced with incredulity.

"It would appear so." I shrug my shoulders, resting my elbows on the surface, steepling my fingers. "Because here you sit, in my office." I let out a small huff, grimacing as I shake my head and continue my train of thought out loud. "As my student."

"But, why?" Her brow creasing in confusion.

"Why, what?" I counter, not sure which part of my life she might be asking about.

"Why are you an escort if you have this?" She waves a hand around my office, her gaze taking in the shelves of books, the white board, a calendar on the wall, the laptop on my desk, before landing back on me.

"I never made it a secret that being an escort was a part time gig, nor that I enjoyed it." I fold my hands in front of me, meeting her stare dead on.

"But, you're a professor. At *Columbia*. One of the best colleges in America." She scrunches her nose up, contempt written on her face. "Isn't that a bit of a conflict?"

"How would it be a conflict if I keep the two separate?" I challenge.

"One is a respected position, and the other, well, the other is seedy!" She exclaims, her brow furrowing.

"You didn't think it was too *seedy* when you wanted me to give you what you needed." My voice dark.

Her face softens, her chin lowering, one side of her mouth tilting down. "Don't spin this around, Xander. Don't turn what happened between us into something dirty."

"You're the one insinuating what happened was dirty." I counter. She's silent, her gaze intent as she continues to assess me. Not sure where to take this conversation, I gage on the side of professionalism. "It's Professor Walker, or if you prefer, Alexander, when we're on this campus." I instruct, making it clear what my role will now be to her, knowing full well I'm being an asshole.

Her posture turns rigid, small creases forming around her eyes as they narrow, her tone venom laced. "So, *Professor*, how do you propose we handle this situation?"

"Which situation would that be, Ms. Knight?" I drum my fingers across the top of my desk before shifting back in my seat. "The fact that we've fucked, that I'm an escort, or that I'm now you're teacher."

Her mouth falls open, forming a small O, and Jesus Christ if it doesn't make me want to rip my zipper open and shove my cock down her throat. She recovers quickly, even if the pink color staining her cheeks defies her confident response. "All of it! How are we supposed to behave?"

I rise, moving around my desk to lean against the space directly in front of her, casually crossing my arms. She clamps her thighs together and shifts her entire body away from me, but continues to meet my eyes with a glare.

"We behave like two adults who had consensual sex. Once." I uncross my arms and bend so my face is inches from hers. "Which will not happen again." Her face blanches as she leans away from me. "I'm your professor. You are my student. If that's too difficult of a concept for you to handle, you are free to drop my class or transfer to another course."

"Why are you being such an asshole?" The words leave her mouth on an exhale, coming out like a whisper, her breath warm and sweet.

The confusion on her face pierces my gut like a knife. Jesus, hurting her is the last thing I want to do. "I'm not trying to be an asshole, Summer, truly."

I sigh, raking a hand through my locks as I straighten to my full height, then look down at her. "What happened between us was-"

I falter here because I want to say special, but that would defeat the point I'm trying to make. "It was a one-time-thing. And if I had known that you were going to be a student of mine, I would have never agreed to our arrangement." Lies I was also trying to get myself to believe. "I would ask you to behave like an adult, respect my personal life, and keep what happened between us, just that, between us."

"Fine." Her eyes lift to meet mine, defeat and sadness swimming in the blue irises. "Anything else, *Professor*?" She pushes her chair back putting distance between us, standing as she does, swinging her bag over her shoulder.

I step back as well, creating an even larger drift, slowly shaking my head. I fucking hate that I'm causing her any kind of pain, but I know, logically, it's the correct thing to do. "No, that's all."

She lets out a snort, her nostrils flaring, muttering several expletives under her breath as she storms out of my office, the door slamming in her wake.

Chapter Eleven

~Summer~

I blink several times, determined not to let a single tear fall from the water brimming at the corners of my eyes. I will not let him get to me. I said goodbye to him over three weeks ago, and was at peace with what had happened between us. Why was I letting this surprise twist bother me now? I know I was just a job to him. Or at least, that's what I kept trying to make myself believe. When he left the money, I thought, maybe, maybe there was something more, but after his silence and now this encounter, I knew with certainty that definitely wasn't the case.

I turn the corner into the main hall, my head down as I try to gather my wits, and slam into a hard body, my book bag falling to the floor.

"Shit." I curse my clumsiness, bending to pick up my bag.

"Summer?"

I swing my head up, my gaze landing on a confused grin. "Blake?" I swoop my bag up and rise. "What are you still doing here?"

"I was going to ask you the same thing." His dimples appearing as his smile widens.

I shake my head, restraining an eye roll, shrugging my shoulders instead. "Just had a question for the professor."

"You angling to be the teacher's pet already?" A soft chuckle leaves him, his statement clearly a joke.

"Hardly." He has no idea how cutting the comment is to me, so I'm sure my stiff tone catches him by surprise as I note his expression change.

"Sorry." He puts his hands in the air between us. "Was totally kidding."

"No, it's fine." I force a smile. "We just don't see eye to eye on some things." I shrug again. "I'm actually going to go over to the registrar's office and see if I can switch into another class."

"What?" His mouth tugs into a frown. "Who will be my lab partner if you switch out?"

I offer a small smile. "I'm sure you'll be just fine, Blake."

"It definitely won't be as interesting without you there." He confesses.

I shuffle my feet, hoisting the strap of my bag over my shoulder. "Well, it was nice to meet you anyway." I nod my head and start to walk away. "Maybe I'll see you around campus."

"Hope so." He drawls, giving me a little wave before heading in the opposite direction.

Thirty minutes later I'm dealt with another blow as my advisor explains switching out of Professor Walker's class isn't an option. He's the only professor that teaches this course, at this level, and it must be taken in order for me to be able to obtain the degree I want.

"Is there an online course, perhaps?" I plead, hoping for an alternative that will keep me out of his class and away from him.

"I'm sorry, Summer." My advisor shakes her head in response. "Is there an issue with the class or the instructor that merits the need for the change?"

I hold back the huff of disdain I want to expel. *Would the fact that we had sex less than a month ago, and being in the same room with him makes me want to do it all over again count?*

"No, no, it's nothing like that." More lies. "It's a conflict with another course I was hoping to take, but it's okay." I concede, dread pooling in my belly like a muddy bog as I realize I have no choice but to face him twice a week. "I'll survive." *I hope.*

It's Friday, and I make an effort to be early to class, already seated at the table I had claimed earlier that week. I am determined to not let being in the same space as *Professor Walker* affect me in any way. We won't discuss the fact that I changed my outfit exactly seven times this morning, couldn't decide if I should wear my hair up or down, and didn't sleep a wink last night. It's still really warm in the city, so I ended up in denim cut-offs and a plain white t-shirt. I was trying to give off an *I don't care about you in the least* vibe. Not sure if I was carrying it off or not.

"I thought that was you." I bring my gaze up to the voice coming from beside me.

"Lily?" I check, having only met her once over the summer at my aunt and uncle's party in the Hamptons.

"Yep." She nods, continuing. "I was almost certain it was you sitting here on the first day of class, but you left to go speak to the professor before I could say hi." I can't help but notice the curiosity in her tone, but before I can answer, Blake's warm voice startles me.

"You're here."

"I am." I shrug. "Couldn't switch out. Guess you're stuck with me."

"No complaints on that front." One side of his mouth cocks up as he slides onto the stool next to me. "You're about the only thing that was going to make this course bearable."

I feel my cheeks heat and shift my attention to Lily and introduce them.

"Don't we have Psych together?" Lily squints, assessing Blake as they shake hands.

"That's why you look familiar." Blake nods in confirmation.

"Where are you sitting?" I ask, sorry I didn't see her on the first day of class so I could have sat with her, but also not sorry, because Blake isn't such a bad partner to have.

"I'm a couple tables back." She points. "And can you believe who our professor is?" She flashes me a conspiratorial grin, continuing, lowering her voice. "I mean, who would have thought? I wonder if anyone else knows what he's been doing in his off time?"

My gaze darts to Blake, whose brow furrows, my eyes widening as they bounce back to Lily with a slight shake of my head. I know there's no way she could have any knowledge of what happened between Xander and I over the summer, but I also don't feel it's right for us to discuss his personal life so openly.

"Definitely something to talk about later?" I half-whisper, hoping she gets my drift.

"Definitely." She smiles demurely. "I should go sit before class starts, but let's get lunch or a coffee sometime, yeah?"

"I'd love that." I smile, happy to be making some friends on campus.

She gives a small wave before walking away. "Nice to officially meet you, Blake."

He gives her a head nod, then turns to me. "Your hair looks cute up like that." He blurts out of left field, fumbling with a pencil. "So, um, since you're here, I was won-"

"Good morning, class." Blake is effectively cut off as Xander, *Professor Walker*, strolls into the room, tossing a leather bag onto the desk as he continues to the podium. "Who's ready for some fun?"

Half the girls in the room giggle in response, but my face remains a mask of steel as I return the stare he has focused on me. What in the actual hell? Didn't he just lecture me on being professional three days ago? He thinks he can toss out a seemingly casual remark like that, which I know is laced with innuendo? I should be used to these games of his. The hot and cold vibes he can't seem to gather under his self-control. Unbelievable.

He flashes the tiniest of smirks, then shifts his focus to scan the rest of the room, launching into a lecture about how physics impact our everyday lives. I'm only half listening, my mind wrestling with how to handle Xander's frustrating behavior. Blake taps me on the arm and I frown, turning to face him.

"The professor asked you a question." He hisses under his breath.

I swing my head to the front of the room. "I'm sorry, can you repeat that?"

His eyes are laser focused on mine; his mouth set in a firm line as he steps out behind the podium to walk closer to me. "No, I'm sorry. Are we boring you, Ms. Knight?"

A tingle sweeps up the back of my neck, every hair rising when he stops directly in front of me, dread pooling in my belly as I gape at him.

"Cat got your tongue?" His gaze flicks down to my mouth for just an instant before darting back to my eyes. "Perhaps you think you're still on summer break in that outfit." His lips purse as he openly scans me from head to toe.

Guess I chose the right outfit. The devil on my shoulder stomps with glee. Somehow, I find my voice and stutter out a response. "No, no. I'm sorry."

Before I can say more, he cuts me off. "Stop saying you're sorry." He shoots me a piercing glare. "The question was, which form of energy do you think is more powerful; Potential or Kinetic?"

"Well, I, ah, think it would depend upon specific scenario's, Sir." My fingers fidget with the corner of my laptop as I wait to see if he's going to interrupt me again. He arches a brow with a tilt of his head, so I continue. "Kinetic energy is due to an object having motion, but what that motion is can determine how much energy. A rollercoaster that is climbing up, instead of down will obviously have much more energy at the bottom of its path. Whereas, Potential energy is based upon position, state or arrangement changes. When changed the amount of energy stored is released, which in some cases are the results of kinetic energy."

I stop here, looking to him for a reaction. He continues to stare at me for what feels like forever, my heart rate dancing a tango as I attempt to maintain a calm façade. The corners of his eyes crinkle as he assesses me, before finally, finally, turning on his heel to stride back to the podium.

"Very good, Ms. Knight." He spins around, his gaze on me for only an instant, before he addresses the class again. "Anyone want to argue that point?" Hands raise around the room, and the focus is finally off of me.

"Holy shit." Blake whispers, leaning closer to me. "Good recovery, Summer."

"You think?" I mumble back, shaking my head in disbelief that anything about that interaction could be construed as good. Thankfully, the rest of the class is uneventful, at least in terms of me being put on the spot. I don't waste a single second when class is dismissed, scooping my laptop into my bag before practically sprinting out of the room, not leaving an opportunity for Xander to make contact with me in any way.

"Summer." I hear my name being called as I exit through the door, but don't stop, fearing the worst, and not wanting to confront it. Him. The man who still haunts me nightly in my dreams, and now my days.

"Hey." A hand clamps around my bicep as I slip out the building doors into the freedom of fresh air and space. I whirl around, expecting to come face to face with Xander, my features softening when instead my gaze lands on Blake.

"Oh, it's you." I breathe out, unable to mask the relief I feel.

"Who else would it be?" I'm met with a frown, his brow scrunched up. "Are you okay?"

"Yes, yes." The corners of my mouth tug up to form what I hope is a convincing smile. "Just have some things on my mind."

He realizes he's still holding my arm, and releases it, nodding his head, I think to placate my response. "You sure?"

"I'm sure." I confirm, forcing a wider grin. "What's up? Did you need something?" Other students brush by us as they exit the building, so I motion for him to move over to the lawn area, out of the way of traffic.

"Uh, yeah, so I was wondering if you were busy tomorrow night?" His cheeks turn the slightest shade of pink. "If maybe you wanted to get a drink, or maybe some dinner?"

"Are you asking me on a date?" I clarify, because honestly, I'm not very experienced in this area.

He chuckles, running a hand over his mouth, then replies sheepishly. "Whatever makes you more comfortable. If not a date, then it's just us hanging out on a Saturday night."

My eyes widen as I'm unable to hide my surprise. "Well, I'm supposed to meet my cousin, Serena, for dinner tomorrow."

"Oh, okay." His foot scuffing the grass, his head tilting down as I notice his disappointment.

"But, um, maybe we could meet you somewhere after for a drink? Our reservation is at seven, so it will still be fairly early when we finish up." I offer in an attempt of consolation.

His eyes light up as they meet mine. "That sounds like a great idea."

"Okay." I nod, smiling. "Let me see what's in the area

around the restaurant and I'll text you an address. Probably be around nine?"

"Perfect." His grin growing even wider. We exchange cell numbers, and then Blake hurries off, explaining he's got another class to get to.

I watch him walk away, then shove my phone in my bag, slinging it over my shoulder, my attention shifting to a lone figure standing just outside the doors of the building. He's as still as a statue, his face an unreadable mask of stone, his eyes focused entirely on me. I glower back, my physical being frozen in place, my mind racing with a million thoughts. I wait a full minute and then take a step in his direction, his response an immediate shake of his head before he swivels to storm back into the building.

What in the actual hell?

Chapter Twelve

~Xander~

That girl will absolutely be the death of me. I'm the one that lectured her on keeping things professional, yet I can't seem to keep my wits whenever she's about. It's her goddamn beauty, her innocence, the way she carries herself with such grace. All without even realizing it, which only makes her more enticing. She's a burning flame and I'm the moth, sparked on by a desire I can't seem to extinguish.

I had hoped she would drop my class, but it seems that isn't going to be the case. It was easy enough to let her go a month ago when I thought I wouldn't see her again. Wouldn't have to stop the dirty thoughts racing through my brain every time I looked at her sensual, full lips and remember what they felt like against mine. How her sweet breath and warm tongue mingled with mine.

How hot her mouth was as she wrapped those same lips around my cock.

"Fuck me." I mutter, my hand moving to adjust that same appendage, twitching under the zipper of my pants. Thank God no one has entered the classroom yet. I made it a point to get here early for once. Even though every cell of my being knows it's wrong, I want to see her walk into the class. I want to be able to have thirty seconds of just watching her. Thirty seconds to see her reaction to me. Thirty seconds to see if and how she looks at me. That thirty seconds will tell me everything I need to know about whether or not she is as obsessed with me as I am of her.

I get my wish, not five minutes later, when she strolls into the room, her face lit up with a bright smile, her attention completely focused on the man walking next to her. Blake Davenport. I should have known this was a possibility from the moment I saw them interacting the first day of class. A fucking Davenport though.

I suppose he was well matched for her financially, but that family is known for being more than a little ruthless with their wealth. She's entirely oblivious to my presence, a soft giggle escaping that luscious mouth as they both take their seats. It occurs to me that perhaps I don't have the impact or effect on her I thought I did. Which also startles me into realizing *she* is the one affecting me. Well, that thirty seconds didn't quite work out the way I thought.

I continue to observe the behavior between them, scrutinizing every smile, laugh, and ugh, touch. Why the fuck is he brushing his fingers against her hand? What exactly transpired between them over the weekend that makes him think he has a right to touch her like that. My body heats as a surge of possessiveness takes hold. I force myself to look away, darting a glance around the rest of the room, noticing it's grown rather full. I need to stop this behavior before someone heeds the inappropriate obsession I have developed.

I rise from my chair, the legs scraping loudly against the wooden floor as it slides back, all eyes in the room training on me. I clear my throat as I stride to the podium, "Let's get started, shall we?"

I spend the next forty-five minutes discussing the behavior of dark matter and energy and how it relates to the nature of fundamental particles. I can't help but note how the subject matter greatly reflects my mood. There's still fifteen minutes left before the class ends, but I don't have it in me to blather on about energy, so surprising even myself, I address the class.

"You can go." I wave my hand dismissively. "I'll see you all on Friday." I steal a glance in the one direction I shouldn't, my spine stiffening as Blake places a hand on Summer's lower back. "Except you, Ms. Knight."

She freezes mid-step, her head tilting to the front of the room, her brow scrunched in confusion as her gaze meets mine.

"I'd like a word with you in my office, please." I don't wait for her to respond, instead pivoting my body to the back of the room to start walking to the rear door. A moment later I hear the patter of steps behind me, so I know she's following.

Neither of us says a word as she waits for me to unlock the door, then hold it open for her to walk through. As soon as she does, I shut it firmly behind me, spinning to face her, shoving my body against hers until her back slams into the wall.

"What the fuck are you doing with Davenport?" My eyes bore into hers, as she gapes open mouthed at me.

It only takes three seconds before she gathers her wits, her expression changing to one of fury as her eyes squint and her nostrils flare out in heat. "How is that any of your damn business?"

She struggles under my hold, trying to slither out from my grasp, my body reacting by pressing into her further. Her eyes flare when she registers the full affect she has on me, a gasp slipping past her lips as she stops wiggling her hips. "Xander?"

"Summer." I practically growl.

"What are you doing?" Her voice timid now, no longer angry. "You're breaking the rules."

"I don't fucking know." I shake my head, stepping back, raking a hand through my hair. "I'm sorry. I shouldn't have done that."

She takes a tentative step in my direction. "I thought you said-"

"I know!" I interrupt, then soften my voice. "I know." I grip the back of my neck and pace around the small space between us. "I just wasn't prepared to have that boy thrown in my face."

"Blake?" She questions, a frown tugging down one side of her mouth for only a moment before it turns up in a smirk, realization dawning. "Oh my God. You're jealous."

"You think I'm jealous?" I huff, attempting to back pedal. "This is not jealousy, this is concern. The Davenport men are known to be ruthless rakes. That boy is not worth your time."

She completely heeds what I say, repeating her earlier conclusion. "You are. You're jealous." Her smile broadens as she crosses her arms over her chest. "Admit it."

I clench my jaw, then blow out a slow breath. "Not jealous, Summer. Protective. You deserve better."

She glances below my waist, a single brow arching as her blue eyes pierce through mine. "Your body would indicate otherwise."

"How my body reacts is of no consequence." I grit out. "It's what he'll try to do to yours that worries me."

"Really?" She moves closer, close enough for me to feel the heat radiating off her body, her floral scent invading my senses. She reaches out and trails her fingers softly over my cheek, down my neck and over my chest.

I clasp my hand over hers, stopping her from moving any lower, my breath hot as I lock my gaze with hers. "You need to stop."

"But why? If this is of no consequence." She smirks, and fuck if it doesn't make my cock jerk in my pants.

"You're playing with fire, Summer, and believe me, neither of us want to get burned." I murmur, my lips only an inch from hers.

"Oh, I don't know." She flutters her lashes as me, lust in her voice. "I've always liked it a little hot." She runs the pink tip of her tongue over her bottom lip, leaving it glistening in its wake. She tilts her head, her full, wet, pouty mouth begging to be kissed.

She's pushing every ounce of restraint I have to the limit, including the bulge throbbing below my waist. I want nothing more than to make that teacher fantasy come true. I want to swipe every last thing off my desk, throw her ass over it and sink myself so deep inside her, she screams my name. But at what cost? My job? My reputation? *Her* reputation? No. I won't do that to her.

Instead, because I can't resist one taste, I brush my lips delicately over hers, and then take three steps back. The disappointment on her face is visible, her cheeks flushing pink, I'm sure in embarrassment. And, because I'm the bastard I am, I don't do anything to lessen it, instead I feed it.

"Still the same little girl, I see? Still not understanding the consequences of your actions."

"My actions?" Her hands clench into fists, her voice hissing like an angry cat. "What about your actions? You're the one that brought me in here! You're the one that pressed me up against the wall! You're the one who's jealous!"

I know she's right, but I'll be damned if I admit it. "I'm not doing this with you, Summer." I wrap a light grip around her forearm and guide her toward the door. "Just heed my warning and stay away from Davenport. He's bad news."

Her eyes turn to thin slits, her response venom. "You're the one that's bad news."

"As long as you remember that, little girl, we'll be just fine." I shove her out the door and slam it behind her before she can say anything else. I fall against it, sliding my hand down my face. I am so thoroughly fucked.

Chapter Thirteen

I stare at the door that just slammed behind me, my blood boiling at his conflicting behavior. One minute he tells me to stay away, and the next, he's shoving his attraction against my waist. I reach out to grab the door handle, deciding I'm not quite done telling him what I think, when a voice startles me.

"What did Professor Walker want?"

I twirl around to find Blake leaning up against the wall across from the door. I can't help but wonder if he heard any of the exchange between us, so naturally, my body betrays me as a hot flush crawls over my skin. Especially being he was the very subject of our conversation.

"Oh, Blake, hi." I struggle to come up with a plausible reason for being pulled into Xander's office, and try diverting the focus to him. "What are you doing here?"

He stares at me in silence, long enough to make me uncomfortable, before he finally pushes off the wall to walk beside me. "I wanted to make sure you were okay."

"I'm fine." I lie. "He knows my aunt and wanted to know if I had seen her recently." I blabber on, weaving a complete fabrication out of thin air. "She hosted some fundraiser and wanted to follow-up on a donation he made."

"Oh, so you already knew the professor?" He surmises, suspicion in his tone.

My step almost falters as I realize this lie is starting to feel like it's snowballing out of control, the next falsity tumbling out of my mouth a little too easily. "No, not really. I've seen him at a couple of my aunt's parties."

"Hmm, interesting." He murmurs.

"Interesting, how?" I push.

"I wonder if that's why he's so hard on you."

"I don't know what you mean?" I tilt my head.

"Just that maybe he doesn't want it to seem like favoritism, since he knows you, so he does the opposite and pushes you instead."

"Yeah, maybe." If he only knew how close to the truth he was.

"I mean, honestly Serena, who does he think he is?" It's a day later and I'm at my aunt and uncle's apartment downtown. They aren't home, both of them off somewhere, doing whatever it is they do during the day.

I'm still fuming, and if I'm honest, a bit thrilled, about the little meeting Xander called me into his office for. I had held out exactly one week after sleeping with Xander before I spilled the whole story to my cousin.

"Well, it's obvious he's attracted to you." She takes a sip of wine from the glass in her hand. "The question is, are you attracted to him?"

"To quote my father, "Does a bear shit in the woods?"". We both giggle before I continue. "You've seen him. He's gorgeous. How could I not be attracted to him? And when he's not being a prick, he's actually pretty nice."

"But?" Serena arches a brow, urging me to reveal my unsaid thought.

"But he's my professor." I finish.

"So, drop the class."

"I can't. I already tried that." I take a sip of my wine. "He's the only teacher that offers the class at that level, and it's a required course for my curriculum."

"It's not like it doesn't happen." She shrugs, her face devoid of any expression. "Professors fuck their students all the time."

"Serena!" I slap her shoulder. "Don't be so crude!"

"What?" One side of her mouth quirks up in a smile.

"It's one of the oldest taboos in the book. And didn't you say you wanted to come to the city to experience life?"

"Well yeah, but I don't want to get thrown out of school!" I retort, holding back a giggle, the wine starting to hit me.

"So don't get caught." She grins like the Cheshire cat.

"You aren't helping to solve my problem one little bit, Serena Ward!"

"You know what you need to do, don't you?" She clicks a fingernail against the side of her glass as her brow furrows in thought.

I stare at her a moment, shaking my head slowly back and forth. "No. But I have a feeling you're going to tell me."

"You need to make him admit he wants you." She states like it's the most obvious thing in the world.

"First, why would I want to do that? And second," I exhale while shaking my head, afraid of what her answer is going to be, "how exactly do I make him admit it?"

"Because, my sweet, innocent cousin, nothing is more satisfying than putting a man in his place, except of course, seeing them pant at what they can't have."

"You lost me." My eyebrows squish together.

"Turn the tables on him, Summer!" She exclaims, a smirk playing over her lips. "We're going to turn you into the sexiest little school girl he's ever seen, and play out every damn fantasy he's probably ever had in that class. You're going to make him so uncomfortable in his need for you that there will be no way for him to deny he wants you."

"Are you crazy, Serena?" I blurt out, taking a large gulp of my wine.

"Well, probably, but that's beside the point." She practically cackles. "But seriously, make him as uncomfortable as he makes you! Give him a taste of his own medicine. Don't let him think he has all the control."

"This just seems like I'd be playing with fire." I retort. "So, I tease him, and then what do I do?"

"Whatever the hell you want." She cocks a naughty grin at me. "You are a grown ass woman, own it."

"Again, there's that whole not getting thrown out of school thing that worries me." I argue.

"Then don't get caught." She purrs, rising out of her chair. "Come on, let's go see what I've got in my closet to slut you up."

"Serena!" I yelp, dashing after her, and not to stop her.

An hour later, as I stare at myself in the mirror, my mouth hanging open, I cannot believe I've let my cousin talk me into this crazy plan.

"Oh, there is no way in hell he's going to be able to take his eyes off you in that outfit."

I turn from the mirror and face her. "Are you sure this is a good idea?"

She tilts her head while lifting her glass. "All's fair in love and war, baby."

Chapter Fourteen

~Xander~

I stride into the classroom, head straight to the podium, tossing my case on the desk as I pass, aware I'm a bit late, but thanking God it's Friday. This has been the longest damn week, and knowing I would be forced to endure Summer sitting in front of me for the next ninety minutes, didn't make it any easier.

I open my mouth to address the class, but freeze in place, my jaw dangling wide, my gaze riveted on the very person who's been haunting my nights. She's in the process of removing a long sweater, revealing what she's wearing, or a more fitting description would be, what she's not wearing; a very short black pleated skirt that is no longer than mid-thigh, black Mary-Janes with pink bobby socks, and a fitted pink cashmere sweater that exposes most of her midriff. And her hair. She's got it braided in two pigtails. She's wearing goddamn fuck me handles.

She's trying to come off as completely blasé, but I know her far too well, her flushed cheeks giving away her discomfort. She tosses the long sweater over the back of her chair before taking a seat, her lashes lifting as her focus lands directly on me, the corner of her mouth tugging up into a slight grin. She sweeps her tongue between her full lips, accentuating the pink gloss already shimmering over them. My brow kicks up. Maybe she's not as trepidatious as I think. At least the smirk she's giving me would indicate otherwise.

This little vixen knows exactly what she's doing. It becomes all too clear when instead of crossing her legs, she spreads them slightly, her fingers tugging the hem of the skirt up just high enough for me to glimpse white cotton panties. My cock stiffens into a hard length, and I thank all that is holy that I'm standing behind this podium. I'm not sure what kind of game she's playing, but this point definitely goes to her. I want nothing more right now than to shred every scrap of clothing from her body and bury myself deep inside her.

I shift, hoping my discomfort isn't obvious to the whole damn class, noticing at the same time that Davenport's tongue is practically hitting the top of the table. God, I hate that fucking guy. He needs to keep his dirty thoughts off my girl.

Whoa. Do I actually have feelings for this girl? I gulp at my own revelation. Why else would another man looking at Summer make me so unreasonably pissed. Jesus, if I wasn't fucked before, I truly am now. She lets out the smallest giggle, her hand leaving her skirt to cover her luscious lips, making me want to take her over my knee and spank her. She knows what this is doing to me and she's enjoying every heinous second.

I close my mouth, realizing it's still open, and glance to the back of the room to see if my teaching assistant is in the class. As if the universe decided I needed one thing going in my favor, I spot him sitting at one of the tables. I give him a discreet nod, hoping my intentions are clear. He rises and starts walking in my direction so I proceed.

"Good morning, class." I try so hard not to, but find myself shooting another glance in Summer's direction. She has the end of her pen in her mouth, her lips closed around the tip, as she pushes and pulls it lazily in and out. I blink, startled by her brazenness, and wonder what kind of monster I've created.

I clear my throat, shifting behind the podium again, and look away from the magnet she's become to me. I smile gratefully when Tim moves to stand next to me. "My T.A., Tim Mathers, will be instructing today's class for you. He'll review the requirements for the first lab you'll be expected to complete by the end of next week."

I hold my hand out to Tim, which he shakes in a firm grip. "It's all yours."

He gives a curt nod, and begins to address the class as I turn abruptly and make my escape out the rear door, not chancing even a parting glance toward the flame that seems to have ignited into an inferno.

I bang on the door to her room with a closed fist for the second time, wondering if she's there and ignoring me, or if she's really not home. After waiting for a full minute and hearing nothing but deafening silence, I exhale a hot breath and conclude she must be out. I jog back down the steps and thrust the door open, the cool night air doing nothing to dampen my temper, still seething and hot after the stunt she pulled in class earlier today.

Where the hell could she be at seven on a Friday night? My step falters as Blake Davenport's face invades my consciousness. Which does nothing to stem the heat already boiling in my veins. She better not fucking be with that twat.

Without thinking, I yank my cell from my pocket, find her number and press call. I'm shocked when I hear her voice on the line, not believing for an instant she would actually answer.

"Hi Professor." Her tone is coy, like she had been waiting for me to phone.

"Where the hell are you?" I grind out, my patience at an all-time low, skipping any niceties.

"What, no hello?" She lets out a small laugh. "What's got you so wound up, Professor?"

"Not even a little bit funny, Summer." I growl, making

it clear I'm in no mood to joke around. "We need to talk. Where are you?"

"Ugh." She grunts. "Talking is so over rated. Can I suggest something way more fun?"

Where in the world had my timid little country mouse gone? I had apparently taught her way more than I realized. "Summer, I'm serious."

"Yes, I know. Way too serious for your own good." Her tone biting. "I don't need another lecture about consequences, so if that's what you have to say, I'm not interested."

"Just tell me where you are so we can meet." I demand. "What's happening in class needs to stop."

"Who-"

Her sentence is cut off by a short cry, and then a loud thunk, and I pull the phone away from my ear to see if she hung up on me. She didn't, so I lean into the phone and call out to her.

"Summer?" I push the phone tighter to my ear and can just barely hear her.

"Here! Take it! There's no money though, just cards."

My heart races as I realize she's being mugged.

"Summer!" I shout into the phone. "Tell me where you are!" All I can guess is that she dropped her phone, because we still seem to be connected. I don't know if she can hear me though. Why didn't she tell me where she was!

I try to listen for any clues, but all I can decipher is someone yelling at her. "Give me those earrings too! Hurry up!" I hear what sounds like a thud, and then a shriek before sobs. Sobs that I know are coming from Summer.

My chest feels like a herd of Mustangs are galloping through the desert, my hand gripping my hair as I shout into my phone again. "Summer, tell me where you are!"

I hear another smack, and then footsteps thundering and then more sobs. "Summer! Summer, are you there? Can you hear me? Find your phone, Baby! Tell me where you are!"

I just keep yelling out, hoping she'll hear me, as I run frantically down the street, not sure which direction to go in.

"Xander?" Her voice, finally, on the other end.

"I'm here." I confirm. "Are you okay? Where are you?"

For a moment all I hear is crying, and a surge of anger so intense has me seeing red. I will kill whomever did this to her. "Summer, baby, can you tell me where you are? I'll come and get you."

She exhales loudly, hiccupping between a sob. "I was at Butler Library, and then I went to Stroko's to get a salad, and I cut through their alley to get to my street."

"Are you in the alley, then?" Christ, that's right down the street from her building. I wasn't more than a thousand feet away! I switch directions and run towards Amsterdam Ave. "I'm coming, Summer!"

"Hurry, Xander. I'm scared." She whimpers. "Don't hang up."

"I won't." I promise. "I'm almost there. Hold on."

I turn and bolt down the alley, skidding to a halt when I see her crumpled on the ground up against a wall. I slide down beside her and gather her into my arms, pulling her close. Her body begins to shake as she melts into me, her sobs vibrating against my chest.

"I've got you now." I murmur into her hair, tugging her onto my lap and off the cold cement. "Shhhh, it's okay."

I hug her closer to me, rubbing my hand in small circles on her back until she seems calmer. Her head is tucked under my chin, her breathing regulating against the bare skin at the open neckline of my shirt. "How you doing now? Any better?"

She peers up at me, her lashes wet with tears, my jaw clenching when I see the red, swelling of a punch under her eye. I lift my fingers and feather them over her cheek, lifting her face to see where else she may have been hit. "Where else are you hurt?"

"After they hit me, and I fell to the ground, they kicked me in my ribs." She moves her hand to show me where. I lift her shirt, and can see an imprint of a bruise already forming on her side. I grimace, my teeth gnashing together as I hold back every dark thought running through my head.

"They?" I inquire softly. "Was it more than one person?"

"No, it was just one." She shakes her head. "But they had on a baseball cap and a hoodie. I couldn't see what they looked like."

"It's okay." I kiss the top of her head. "You're safe now."

"I'm so stupid. I should have never gone through the

alley." She shakes her head under my hold. "I just wanted to get home and eat. I was so hungry. And I wasn't paying attention because I was talking to you on the phone."

"All that matters right now is that you're okay." I scoff. "Relatively speaking."

"They took my bag. It has all my stuff." She pulls back from me, her brow scrunched with worry. "My laptop, my credit card, my I.D.'s. My keys!" Her face becomes a shade of white. "They will know where I live!"

"Can you stand?" I check, and she nods. "Come on, let's get up then."

We both rise, her legs shaking under her as we do, so I wrap a hand around her waist to steady her. "I have a friend who's dating a detective. I'm going to call her and have him help us, okay?"

"Okay." She replies meekly.

She leans against me, quiet as I call Gabby and explain what's happened. I end the call a few moments later and update Summer.

"Gabby and Cameron are on their way. We're lucky, Cameron was just picking up Gabby up from work at the hospital, so they're close."

Chapter Fifteen

~Summer~

Twenty minutes later, we're walking into Xander's apartment, and I heave out a sigh of relief I didn't know I was holding. I'm safe.

"Come on." Xander's friend Gabby wraps a hand around my shoulder and guides me to the couch. "Let's get you warm." She covers me with a blanket that was thrown over the back of a chair, pulling it tight to cocoon me. She lifts my chin, her multi-colored eyes examining my face. "Were you hit anywhere else besides your cheek?"

I nod and explain how I was kicked.

"Let me see." She offers me a kind smile. "I don't know if Xander told you, but I'm a nurse. I just want to make sure nothing is cracked or bleeding."

"Okay." I unfold the blanket and lift my shirt to expose my side. I'm so thankful I went home and changed into leggings and a sweatshirt after class today. If they had seen what I was wearing earlier, they probably would have assumed I deserved to be mugged. She presses against the raised skin, already bruising along my ribs, and I grimace.

"I know." She soothes, pressing her hand flat against the wound. Her kind eyes meet mine. "Something similar happened to me, so believe me when I say I understand every single thing you're feeling right now."

I nod, tears springing to my eyes again, and whisper that I'm okay.

"You aren't." She lowers my shirt and gazes into my eyes. "And that's alright too. Let yourself feel everything you need to. No one here is going to fault you for that." She pats my hand. "I don't believe anything is cracked, but we can certainly bring you to the hospital for an X-ray if you'd like?"

"No." I shake my head forcefully. "I don't want that."

"Okay." Her lips form a tight line. "If you change your mind, or start feeling worse, you tell me."

I nod again, then direct my attention to Xander, who is a few feet away, speaking in a hushed voice to Cameron. "I should call my aunt, or my cousin. They can come and get me."

"Absolutely not." He strides over, his features stern. "You're not going anywhere. I want you here where I know you're safe."

Gabby darts a questioning look Xander's way, and then towards Cameron, and I know she's trying to figure out what our relationship must be. I wish I had an answer to that very question. She rises from the couch and walks toward the kitchen.

"Xander, I'm sure I'll be quite safe at my aunt and uncle's apartment." I try to assure him.

He sits beside me, brows drawn together as he slides one of my hands into his. "That may be, but I would feel better with you here. In my care and able to see for myself that you're safe."

I tilt my head, biting my lower lip as I study him. As usual, his behavior leaves me in a state of confusion. His actions saying one thing, his words usually another, but this time, his feelings seem entirely clear.

"I'm not your responsibility." I murmur. "You don't have to take care of me."

"I want to." His blue eyes lock onto mine. "Please, let me do this for you."

I blink several times, then dip my head, breaking the hold he has on me as I murmur my acceptance. "I should at least call them and let them know what's happened."

"Let's do that in the morning." He stands. "After you've had a good night's rest and a report has been filed." He turns to Cameron. "What do you need from Summer?"

Before he can reply, Gabby is back and takes charge. "What Summer needs is rest." She reaches out and places an ice pack in my hand. "He only had one in his freezer, but I'd switch it between your cheek and your side to help reduce the swelling and the bruising."

She points to Xander. "Do you have some ibuprofen, Xanax, or some wine?"

"I've got bourbon." He scratches his chin. "Definitely some Advil, but no wine or narcotics." He cocks his head at Gabby. "Are you sure we should be giving her anything? What if she's bleeding internally?"

"Oh, for Christ's sake, Xander, she's not bleeding internally." She huffs and rolls her eyes. "You're going to scare the poor girl to death." She turns to me. "You got a good whack on your cheek and side, but I'm quite sure you aren't in any danger of bleeding out on us." She swings her gaze back to Xander. "When did you become so dramatic?" She flings a hand out. "Go get the Advil and whatever you have to drink."

"You're so goddamn bossy." He grumbles, stalking out of the room.

"Try living with her, man." Cameron jests, flashing a quick smile Gabby's way, then moves closer to me. "We can talk tomorrow, Summer. Alexander has filled me in on what happened, the fact that you couldn't see the perpetrator's face, or anything else that might be helpful in identifying the mugger."

I bow my head, my shoulders slumping. "I'm sorry I'm not being more helpful."

He places a hand on my shoulder. "You've got nothing at all to apologize for. You're the victim here and haven't done anything wrong." He squeezes gently. "Remember that, okay?" He takes a step back, releasing his hold.

"And remember, you are completely safe here. Alexander will take good care of you."

I tip my head up so I can look him in the eyes. "Thank you."

"Of course." He gives a firm nod. "Oh, when you can, make sure you call your credit card companies and let them know they've been stolen. Also, let the school know, as well as your landlord. I can have Gabby text Alexander the number of a locksmith to get your locks changed as soon as possible. I'm not sure if there's anything we'll be able to do about your laptop. Those are usually wiped immediately." He frowns. "I'm sorry about that."

Shit, I had temporarily forgotten about my keys. "Do you think they will try and break into my room? I have things there that are valuable. Some money and jewelry." My voice begins to shake when I think about the possibility of a stranger in my room, going through my belongings, taking my things.

"Why don't you write down your address for me?" He retrieves a small pad and a pen from his jacket pocket and hands it to me. "I'll take a ride over to see if anyone's attempted to enter your room, and I can also speak with the building supervisor to see if we can manage who comes in and out of the building tonight."

"Okay." I nod, and write my address, as well as my cell number on his pad then hand it back. "Thank you again for all your help."

"Please, there's no need for thanks. I'm glad we were close and able to help." He reads what I've written and then stores the pad back in his pocket, turning as Xander appears. He's carrying a tumbler filled with ice and brown liquid in one hand, and a couple orange pills in another.

"Do you even like bourbon?" He kneels in front of me, holding out the Advil. "Or should I get you some water?" His shoulders slump. "I'm sorry I don't have much here to offer to drink." He lifts one side of his mouth up in an attempt at a smile as he shrugs. "Wasn't expecting company."

"Is it good bourbon?" I scoop the pills out of his hand, toss them in my mouth, and then take the glass from the other and take a large swallow.

His brow kicks up, the other side of his mouth rising to display a broader smile. "It's a Blanton's single barrel."

I hum in appreciation as the liquid travels down my throat and into my stomach, leaving a warm trail of heat in its wake. "Not bad."

He chuffs. "Well, aren't you full of surprises?"

"My dad loves a good bourbon." I explain. "He may have let me sample from his collection from time to time."

He stares at me, long enough that my heart beat flutters and I feel my body begin to ignite, Gabby finally speaking, breaking the contact between us.

"We're going to go to Summer's place to see if anyone has tried to get in." She has her hand in Cameron's, her gaze shifting back and forth between Xander and I, scrutinizing our interaction.

"Thank you for everything." Xander stretches to his full height and steps over to Cameron to shake his hand,

and then kiss Gabby on the cheek. "Call me and let me know what you find?"

"Of course." Cameron confirms.

Xander walks them to the door, shutting and locking it behind them once they leave. I watch as he makes his way back to me, his hand raking through his hair as he does. "What do you need? A shower? Food? Do you want to climb into bed?"

My brows arch, and I almost choke on the sip of bourbon I'm taking.

"Oh, no!" He stammers. "I didn't mean like that." His fingers thread through his locks again, leaving them a disheveled mess. "Are you tired? You can go lie down in my bed. Alone." He clarifies.

I laugh, because at this point, it's that or cry, and seeing him nervous for once, completely puts me at ease.

He stops pacing. "You're laughing?"

"You're funny." I declare.

"I'm funny?" He parrots, his eyes creasing as they narrow. "How?"

"You're always so in control." I tease, unable to hide my smile. "You're so jittery right now. So unsure what to do with me."

"This is uncharted territory for me, Summer." His tone gruff. "It's not common practice for me to have an ex-client, current student, now also a damsel in distress in my apartment."

"Damsel in distress?" I scoff. "I'm no princess, and this certainly is no fairy tale."

"I'm no fucking prince charming, that's for sure." He

finally smiles, his fingers brushing against mine as he snags the tumbler from my hand, lifting it to his mouth to take a long swig.

"I'm starving." I blurt. "If you want to know what I need." I put my hand on my grumbling stomach. "I need some food. That damn thief threw my salad on the ground."

"Food I can do." He takes another drink from the glass, hands it back to me, then holds up a finger. "Be right back."

A minute later he's back with a stack of take-out menus. "Pick whatever you want." He lays them on the table in front of me, fanning them out so I can peruse the choices. And for the first time since we've walked through the door, I really look at him.

He's wearing a white button-down dress shirt over a pair of worn jeans and a pair of loafers. The top of the shirt is unbuttoned, leaving the collar loose revealing a dusting of chest hair. It's simple, but on him it's anything but. He could make a paper bag look appealing. I chew on my bottom lip, scanning him from head to toe, remembering just how delicious the view of that torso is without a shirt.

"Don't look at me like that, Summer." He growls, my attention shifting to his eyes, dark and dilated as they stare back at me. "A look like that will get you into more trouble than either of us needs right now."

I let the blanket slide off my shoulders as I arch my back to sit straighter. Suddenly, every thought of what happened earlier tonight is gone, and all I can think about is Xander. His lips, his touch, the heat of him against me, and it's all I want. I stand and walk to him, his face a mix of emotions.

"Summer, no." His words express rejection, but his tone, the way he's leering at me, indicate the opposite.

I stop in front of him, laying my hand against his chest. His heart beats erratically under my palm, his body warm, even through the material of his shirt. I snap my eyes to his, and breathe out my request. "Please."

"No." He maintains, his tongue darting out to run along his lower lip, his gaze slipping to my mouth. "We can't. It's wrong."

"We can." I coax, moving so I'm only an inch from him. "I just want to forget for a little while. And no one has to know."

"I'll know, Summer. I'll know." His breath warm as it mingles with my own, the slightest hint of the bourbon lingering between us.

"Don't make me beg." I plead, because begging to get what I want doesn't feel beneath me at this very moment.

"Fuck it." Words I don't decipher until his lips are smashed against my own, one hand grasping the back of my neck, the other around my waist as he hauls me flush. I groan, and he takes full advantage, his tongue invading, dueling with mine, our teeth clacking together as we both fight for possession of the other.

"Yoo-hoo!" A female voice suddenly sounds from the doorway. "Alexander, are you home?"

We wrench apart from one another, both of us panting, both of us looking wide-eyed towards the entryway.

I whip my head back to Xander. "Who in the hell is that?"

He never once mentioned he might be seeing anyone. Especially someone who would have a key to his apartment.

"My mother." He deadpans, a scowl appearing before he storms off in her direction.

Chapter Sixteen

~Xander~

"Mother." I stride over to greet her, brushing a quick kiss against her cheek. "What are you doing here?"

"Well, hello to you too." She chuffs, clearly annoyed with my reception.

"Sorry." I offer. "It's been a night."

"I tried calling and texting before coming over." She shrugs off the light jacket she's wearing and hands it to me. "But when you didn't show at the restaurant, your father and I got worried."

"Shit." I close my eyes, pinching my forehead. "I totally forgot we were having dinner tonight." I hang her jacket on a hook across from the door. "I'm so sorry. A friend needed my help and I got completely distracted." I glance behind her. "Where's dad?"

"He took a car back to our apartment." She walks toward the main living space, her brow arching when she notices Summer sitting on the couch. She twists her head my way. "Your friend?"

"She was mugged earlier." I explain.

"What?" Her pace quickens as she makes her way over to Summer. "You poor dear. Are you okay?"

Summer's eyes widen at my mother's approach, her focus bouncing back and forth between us. "Um, yes?"

"You aren't." My mother declares, raising her fingers to brush against Summer's cheek. "Does it hurt?"

"I'm okay." Summer reassures her. "Xander is taking good care of me."

"Did he tell you to call him that?" She scrunches her nose in deference. "I prefer Alexander."

"Oh." Summer glances at me, confusion written on her face.

I interrupt, trying to end the misery my mother's putting her through. "Mother, this is Summer Knight." He motions to me, and then to her. "Summer, meet my mother, Cordelia Walker."

"It's nice to meet you, Mrs. Walker." Summer offers her a tentative smile.

"Please, call me Delia. Mrs. Walker is so formal." She gives Summer's shoulder a soft pat. "So, how do you two know each other?" She glances back and forth at us.

Before Summer can reply, I respond. "She's actually the Ward's niece. I met her in the Hamptons at one of their soirees."

"Sophia and Nick?" She hums her surprise, a smile

appearing as her eyes light up. "Are you Susanna's daughter?"

"You know my mom?" Summer's head tilts to the side.

"I'm a little older than her, but we were in the same sorority at Brown." She explains. "I haven't seen her in years. I think Sophia told me your parents were hiding out in the country somewhere?"

"In Vermont, yes." Summer nods, one side of her mouth kicking up. "They like to stay under the radar."

She turns to Xander, crossing her arms, a smug expression on her face. "Well, you two would certainly make a good match. We could be energy and communication magnates."

"Mother!" I admonish. "We're just friends." I can't help but notice Summer's brows squish together at my mother's comment.

"Uh-huh." She murmurs, her eyes darting back and forth between Summer and I, a gleam I've witnessed one too many times before sparking to life.

"Alright," I wrap an arm around her back. "Now that you know I'm alive and well, time for you to be off, Mother."

"Tell your parents I said hello." She wiggles her fingers over her shoulder as Xander guides her away. "And nice to meet you, Dear."

"Mom, stop trying to play matchmaker anytime you see me with a woman." I shush out, snagging her jacket to hold it open for her.

"What?" She rolls her eyes. "You're thirty-two,

Alexander. You've got to start thinking about these things."

"Mother, I'm fine." I herd her toward the door. "Thank you for checking on me. I'll call you tomorrow to reschedule dinner. Please send dad my apologies."

"Oh, speaking of your father, one of the things he wanted to speak to you about tonight was the annual board meeting. He wanted to confirm you would be attending." She stops in the doorway. "This is important, Alexander. He's not going to be able to run the company forever. He's approaching sixty-five."

I scrape a hand through my hair, exhaling a long breath before speaking. "Mother, I'm a professor. I don't want to be CEO of the company. Dad and I have talked about this. I'll serve on the board, but we need to groom someone else for that position. I thought I'd already made that clear."

"Well, you know your father." She muses before leaning forward to kiss my cheek. "I'll tell him you'll be at the meeting."

"Is the Block Island house still open?" I toss out at the last minute.

"Actually, it is, but I've let the staff go for the season." She purses her lips as she stares at me.

"I might go for a couple days if that's okay." I ask.

"Of course." One brow arching. "Alone?"

"Good bye, Mother." I give her a slight shove over the threshold, blow her a kiss and shut the door, heaving a sigh of relief. I lean my forehead against the coolness of the wood for a moment to gather my wits. It's been a night so far, and it's only half past eight. I blow out a breath as I straighten, and stroll back to the living area.

Summer's not on the couch, and a quick scan of the room doesn't reveal where she is. Maybe she went to the restroom? I decide a refill of bourbon is in order, and snag the glass off the table as I make my way to the kitchen.

After sipping on my drink for several moments, without Summer reappearing, I go off in search of her. My apartment isn't very big, hosting the main living area, a bedroom and a bathroom, so it doesn't take long for me to discover her.

I push the bedroom door open, the light from the living area shining a beam onto the bed where a small ball shape is formed. I move closer, confirming it's Summer, curled up tight, her breathing shallow and steady as she sleeps. It's no wonder. I'm sure between the stress of the attack and the bourbon, her mind and body finally gave in to exhaustion.

I take a step back, my focus entirely on Summer. It looks like she made herself at home, noticing she's changed into one of my t-shirts. She must have looked through my drawers until she found one. It's long enough on her that it covers her up to mid-thigh, and I can't help but think it looks pretty damn good on her.

I gather the plush blanket folded on the end of the bed, using it to cover her. She lets out a small, content sigh as her body relaxes under the weight of the material. Her long, blonde hair fans out behind her, no longer in those silly pigtails. I shake my head, accompanied by a slight eye roll, as I recall the outfit she was wearing in class. My dick jerks under the constraint of my jeans, and I shift it back into place, frustration reigning supreme at how my body reacts at just the thought of her.

I continue staring down at her, scratching at the rough stubble on my chin as I consider my options with her. I'd be lying to myself if I try to claim I'm not attracted to her. My body's reaction is a constant reminder of that fact. But it's more than my attraction to her. I genuinely enjoy being in her company, and missed her smart mouth and naivety at the same time. I like that she doesn't try to conform like a lemming, and instead marches to her own beat. She acts on instinct alone, no filter, and that is completely refreshing after the many fake people I encounter on a regular basis.

She's the only woman I've ever had in my bed. The thought dawns on me as I continue to stare at her. It also occurs to me that I like her there. Which is definitely a first for me as well. I'd love to climb in beside her, but I don't want to send her any more mixed signals than I already have. Why in the fuck did she have to walk into my class-room? Anyone else's, but not mine.

I finally pull myself away, treading lightly so I don't disturb her, leaving the door ajar in case she wakes and needs something. I toss the rest of the contents in my glass down my throat, fire scorching a path to my empty stom-ach. I realize we never did eat. I make a mental note to feed her a full breakfast when she wakes. I get comfy on the couch with a book, and dig in, hoping I'll tire out enough to fall asleep. Of course, as soon as I gather the blanket around me, all I can smell is her. She invades my senses, even when she's not near me. She's become my heaven and hell and doesn't even realize it. I need to decide if I want to be the sinner or the saint.

Chapter Seventeen

~Summer~

I blink awake, heat enveloping my back, as my mind catching up as I remember I'm at Xander's. I try to sit up, but an arm tightens around my waist, its owner tugging me closer. My heart accelerates into over-drive, as I sneak a peek over my shoulder to confirm, yep, it's him. Not that I was expecting anyone else. I just certainly didn't peg him as a snuggler.

It's clear he's still asleep by the soft snores escaping him, but I'm not sure what I should do. He mumbles, his waist pushing into my bottom, my mouth forming into a big 'O' as it becomes clear he's sporting some serious morning wood. I try and scoot my middle forward, which results in him dragging me back, with more unintelligible mumbling coming from him as he grinds into me.

Shit. Heat pools between my legs. I clench my lower lip between my teeth as I ponder what my next move should be. Before I have time to figure it out, his hand starts to drift up my stomach and curls around my breast. *Double-shit.* His fingers caress over the top of my nipple, now starting to turn into a hard peak. *Is he seriously doing this in his sleep?* His breathing is still even and shallow, his exhales warm against my neck where his face rests.

My body reacts blindly, my back bowing into his cupped hand, an unconstrained moan tumbling from me. His grip tightens as his hips thrust forward, his lips hot and firm, suddenly pressing into my neck. His length throbs against my ass, my skin flushing at my increased pulse, my hips grinding back into his.

A soft moan vibrates against my neck, and my center clenches in response, my body and my mind falling under his spell. I twist my head and seal my mouth over his, fireworks exploding under my lids at the contact. My body follows suit, turning, my bare legs tangling with his jean clad legs as I wrap my arms around his head to kiss him harder. His tongue sweeps inside, and I swear, I can taste hints of the smoky flavor of the bourbon we drank last night.

I've dreamt of being in his arms again for the last month, but it's nothing compared to the real thing. His mouth slides off mine and begins to trail down my chin, peppering small kisses in a path towards my neck.

"Xander," I pant, as he moves lower, his body freezing at the sound.

He sits up abruptly, his hair askew, eyes flaring wide as recognition seems to occur. "Summer!"

"Xander?" I whisper.

"What are you doing?" He scoots back on the bed, putting space between us.

"What am I doing?" I mimic, feeling like a parrot. I can feel my face coloring in embarrassment at his rejection. "What are *you* doing? You're the one who was wrapped around me when I woke up!"

His gaze darts around the room as if the answer lies somewhere in the periphery, then back to me. "I'm sorry." He stutters, shoving himself up and off the bed, his arousal still apparent. "I couldn't get comfortable on the couch, so I came in here to sleep." He crosses his arms over his chest. "Just sleep." He reiterates. "I didn't mean for that—" He waves a hand over the bed where I'm sitting, "to happen. My body was on auto-pilot."

I frown. "Why are you fighting this so hard? It's not like we haven't already slept together? The rules have already been broken. You obviously want me as much as I want you." I dare to nod to his swollen length, still bulging under his jeans.

"You know why." His tone firm. "You are my student now. You weren't then."

"I'm a god damn adult. Then and now." I retort. "Not a child in high school, or even college. This is graduate school. I think at this point we're mature enough to understand consent and all that it implies."

He's silent for what feels like forever. "It's against the

University's policy for a professor, to sleep with a student, no matter their age."

"So?" I shrug, challenging him. "You're suddenly the prince of morality?" I cock my head. "We both know better."

He lets out a growl, an actual growl, his head falling back onto his shoulders. "Do you think this is easy for me?" His deep blue gaze locks onto mine, desperation in his voice. "I'm trying to do the right thing here, Summer." He shakes his head. "And believe me, it doesn't happen often, but you deserve more than me."

"Why don't you let me decide who and what I deserve?" I chide. "The only thing wrong here is the fact that you continue to treat me like a child." My hands clench into fists. "Like a little girl." I remind him of his favorite nickname for me, my mouth in a grimace.

"You are most definitely not a little girl." He grumbles.

"Then stop treating me like one." I plead.

"Summer, what exactly is it that you want from me?" He paces a few steps closer to the bed. "Sex or a relationship? Because, I don't do relationships. I haven't in a very long time."

"I assumed sex was the only option." I state, doing my very best to look him straight in the eye with all the fake confidence I can muster.

"And therein lies the problem." He scoffs, shaking his head, pacing again. "You aren't the kind of girl to have casual sex, Summer. Especially with the likes of someone like me." He chuffs again for good measure. "No matter what you may try to make yourself believe."

"I believe I'm perfectly capable of having sex without a relationship." I defend.

His nostrils flare, one side of his mouth curling into a feral grin. He prowls around the end of the bed, his eyes gleaming and dark as he stares at me, stopping when he's directly beside me. He leans down, his hands landing on each side of me, his arms caging me in, his face an inch from mine. I rear back until my head hits the pillow, a small gasp of shock escaping me. He looms over me, staring at me with an intensity that has me fidgeting beneath him, the heat from his body radiating.

"Is this what you want?" He taunts, closing the last inch between us, using his teeth to nip my bottom lip, his tongue swiping over the sting. I whimper in delight. His eyes dart to mine, as I nod my consent.

"Say it." He demands. "Tell me you want me to fuck you."

I inhale a sharp breath, then stammer out my plea, feeling like a beggar. "I, I want you to have sex with me."

He shakes his head, eyes hardening as he pushes away from me. "You can't even say the word fuck, let alone handle me doing it to you." He stares down at me, blinking twice, his mouth set in a firm line. "Get dressed. You need to eat something."

"But—" I protest, but he puts a hand up.

"Enough." He turns and storms out of the room. "Enough for now, Summer."

I stare dumbfounded as the door slam shut behind him. At a loss, I do as he instructed and get dressed, pulling on the leggings I was wearing last night, but leave his t-shirt on. It's comfy and it smells like him. I check my reflection in the mirror hanging on a far wall, trying to tame my hair, staring at the bruise on my cheek. I need an elastic, but of course, without my bag, I have nothing. I guess I should consider myself lucky that I at least still have my phone, and only this bruise. It could have been so much worse.

I realize I need to pee, so creep out of the bedroom as quietly as I can and tip-toe to the bathroom. I can smell food cooking, and my stomach grumbles in response. I hate that he was right. Again. I am starving and need food. I go to the bathroom, do my best to cleanup with the supplies he has over his sink, and then venture to the kitchen.

He pauses when he sees me, his gaze sweeping down my body, one corner of his mouth crooking down as his nostrils flare.

"What did I do now?" I glower back at him.

He shakes his head. "Nothing. Come sit." He motions to one of the stools at the breakfast bar.

I sit, and he slides a plate of scrambled eggs and toast in front of me. Steam is still rising off the eggs, the scent heavenly to my empty belly. "Thank you." I smile over at him.

"Do you need more Advil?" His fingers reach out for my cheek, but fall short of brushing it. "I'm sorry this happened to you."

"I'm okay." I offer a shrug. "And it was my own fault. I shouldn't have gone down the alley. I know better."

"If they find who did it, I'll kill them." He snarls, my eyes popping wide.

"Xander-." I start, not really sure how to respond to his statement. He just nods, turning away. "Coffee?"

"Yes, please." I answer, happy to change the subject, shoveling a forkful of the eggs onto a piece of toast before taking a huge bite. I hum in appreciation. "Yum."

He chuckles, a small smile finally gracing his face, only adding to his beauty, and my heart does a little flip. Yeah, sure I can have sex with no attachments. Who am I kidding?

"Cream or sugar?" He lifts the mug in question.

"Both." I manage between bites. I can't seem to stop eating. I smile in gratitude when he places the cup in front of me. "Aren't you having something?"

"This works for me for now." He lifts his coffee. "I usually don't eat until later in the day."

I scan his body and can't help but wonder if that's how he stays so lean. His hair is all rumpled, making him look even sexier, my mind starting to drift off to places it shouldn't.

"Stop looking at me like that." Xander grumbles, striding out of the kitchen.

I shrug, more to myself. I can't help it if he's eye candy. I'm hungry. I chuff out loud at my own thoughts, startled when Xander is suddenly standing beside me.

"Here." He sets an open computer in front of me. "I know your laptop was taken, but you can use mine to contact your credit card company and whomever else about your stolen property."

"Thank you, Xander." I state sincerely. "That's really nice of you."

"I can be nice." He mutters, walking away, then stops, his back still to me. "Can you do me a favor?"

My brow kicks up in curiosity. "If I can."

"Call me Alex or Alexander." He twists his head to glance back at me. "Xander is for work."

Chapter Eighteen

~Alexander~

I trudge forward, without waiting for a response, into the bathroom, shutting the door behind me. I need a shower. A cold one. She's getting under my skin, and I think I'm about to do something I can't quite believe I'm going to do. Before I can analyze and overthink my decision to death, I strip out of my clothes, turn on the shower, and step under the spray.

It takes a second for the water to heat, and I groan at how good it feels. I close my eyes, immersing my head, soaking my hair and my face. When I open my eyes, she's there, hovering in the doorway, her nipples pebbled under my t-shirt. I wait to see what she's going to do, my dick twitching when she slides her leggings off before yanking the shirt over her head, dropping it to the floor.

She's naked and even more beautiful than I remember.

I reach down and grip the base of my cock, squeezing hard as she walks toward me, her gaze locked on mine. She steps in the shower, and then under the falling water. She tilts her head back, running her hands over her hair, flattening the long, wet strands down her back. Rivulets of water stream over her shoulders, between her breasts and down her flat stomach.

I cup a breast in my palm, swiping my thumb over its peak, eliciting a moan from her cloud-like lips. I lean forward to kiss her, our mouths melting together under the torrent of water, our breath becoming one. Her fingers stroke down my length, wrapping around its girth when she reaches the head. She peels her mouth from mine, using her tongue to blaze a trail down my chest and stomach before licking the tip of my cock.

I watch, my eyes hooded, as she opens wide and slides her hot mouth over my length, swallowing when I hit the back of her throat.

"Fuck." I hiss, my hips jerking forward. "Summer." Her name tumbles from me on an exhale of pure ecstasy. She continues to suck me in and out, gliding up and down my shaft, my balls tightening after only a minute.

"I'm going to come." I warn, yanking back, fisting my throbbing cock, my cum spurting as I aim it all over her gorgeous tits. She takes every bit of it, her knees on the floor, her head thrown back as her eyes meet mine, her lips swollen and dark pink. My hand slams against the shower wall to hold myself upright. Deep, heavy pants huff out of me, my heart galloping in my chest.

"Xan-" There's a knock on the bathroom door, startling

me. "Sorry, Alexander. Did you call me? I thought I heard my name."

My eyes spring open, reality interrupting fantasy. I've still got my cock in a vise-grip, and release it as I call out. "I'm fine. I'll be out in a minute." *Unless you want to come in here and help me take care of this.* I keep that last wish to myself, not wanting to invite more trouble than I'm already in.

Five minutes later, with a towel trapped around my waist, I leave the confines of the bathroom for my bedroom. I spy her sitting on the couch, gnawing on her bottom lip as she concentrates on the laptop in front of her. She peeks up at me, her cheeks turning a light pink as she quickly focuses back on the screen. If she only knew what was going through my mind, her cheeks would be more than flushed.

I throw on a pair of jeans and soft, light blue t-shirt. It's the beginning of October, but we seem to be having one last surge of summer, the weekend's weather predicted to be in the high seventies. I run my fingers through my hair to tame it, and exit my room.

"I have an idea."

Her head pops up. "Okay."

"Why don't you come to Block Island with me for the weekend?" I blurt before common sense catches up with me and I change my mind.

Her head cocks, her brow furrowing. "You're asking me to go away with you?"

"It's the holiday weekend. We don't have to be back at school until Tuesday. And I called the locksmith earlier, and they can't get in to change your locks until then at the earliest. So, I figured, why not take advantage? It might be nice for you to get away from the scene of the crime." I rush out. "So to speak."

"What's in Block Island?" She inquires, her brow still scrunched.

"My family has a house there." I try to leave it at that, but of course she presses for more.

"Oh yes, that reminds me. I wanted to ask you about that last night after your mom left, but got side-tracked." She taps her chin. "Something about us being magnates. What exactly do your parents do?"

I blow out a long breath because I know what I'm going to say next is going to prompt ten more questions. "My family owns Walker Communications."

Her mouth slackens, eyes popping wide as she regards me. "Wait. Your family? As in you too?"

"Technically." I shrug. "I'm on the board. I have a salary, and a trust. It's not a big deal."

"I beg to differ." She snorts. "Walker Communications is the biggest media conglomerate there is." She shakes her head. "I don't understand."

"What don't you understand?" I mimic, my patience already running thin.

"If you're rich, and don't say you aren't," she proceeds to roll her eyes dramatically, "why did you need to work as an escort to pay for school? Were you lying? And why are you a professor instead of working for your family?"

"I wanted to make it on my own." I state, not without a bit of sarcasm. "I felt like I had to prove that I didn't need my parents' money or influence. I was young, immature, not even remotely as smart as I thought I was."

"But you're still an escort." Her nose scrunches up as her eyes squint.

"Technically." I drawl, not sure how much more I want to share with her.

"You are or you aren't, Alexander." She cocks her head. "Kind of like my virginity. Remember?"

"Don't you know it's not polite to throw people's words back at them?" I retort, with my own eye roll. "If you must know, I haven't booked an engagement through Temptations since June."

"Since June?" Her lips purse in thought, her eyes widening when realization dawns. "Since you met me?" She whispers.

"Don't let it go to your head." I order. "There were many factors that went into making that decision."

"Uh-huh." She smiles sheepishly. "If you say so." She pauses and then speaks. "I can go and stay with my aunt and uncle for the weekend. You don't have to babysit me."

"I'd like you to come with me." I grip the back of my neck, cursing under my breath before I continue. I don't want to come off like I'm desperate. "We'd be off campus." I meet her gaze trying to be clearer. "No rules."

"Oh." Her fingertips turn white as she clutches the computer on her lap. "I, um, okay." She fidgets in her seat, glancing away from me before looking back at me. "Okay, then."

"Good." I flash her a genuine smile. "I'm glad that's

settled." I gesture to the laptop. "When you're done, we can go to your room and gather what you need. We can call Cameron and give him a status as well."

"Okay." She nods, chewing her luscious lip to a pulp. I finally found a way to keep her quiet. I chuckle. I'm either making the biggest mistake of my life, or the best decision ever. She's invaded my every thought for the last three months. It's time for me to figure out if she's just a temporary obsession or, as scared as hell as I am to admit it, becoming a part of my heart.

Chapter Nineteen

"We're taking that?" I gape at the helicopter whirring to life in front of me.

"It's the best way to get there." Alexander states. "We'll be there in less than thirty minutes. If I drive, it will take over five hours."

"And you tried to pretend you're not rich." I scoff, still trying to absorb and process the new information I learned about Alexander this morning.

We spoke with Cameron, and also stopped at my room. It didn't look like anyone had attempted to break in, so that was a relief. I changed, packed a small bag of my things, and also moved my valuables to a lock box that I hid in the back of my closet. The manager was monitoring who came in and out of the building, so hopefully everything would be fine, but I know you could never be sure.

"Come on." He wraps one hand around the back of my neck, tugging my body to his, brushing a kiss across my lips before moving them to my ear. "I'll keep you safe."

I peek up at him under my lashes, my knees practically giving out under me as I try not to swoon. "I know you will." I whisper back.

He kisses me on the forehead, his hot grip releasing my neck to slide down and grasp my hand. He leads me across the heliport, passing off our bags to the co-pilot, before assisting me into the helicopter. He straps me in, an unmistakable glint in his eye as he does it, which has the butterflies in my stomach flapping overtime. He places a headset over my ears before doing the same to himself, then buckles himself in.

"You'll be able to hear any of us speak in these." He explains, tapping on the gear.

I nod, my pulse picking up speed as the co-pilot climbs into his seat, our ascent starting a moment later. I blow out a breath, trying to stem the flutter of nerves cascading in my belly as I watch the ground disappear under us. Warm fingers wrap around my own, our palms aligning with a gentle squeeze.

"I got you." His voice soothes through the headphones. My eyes dart to his, noticing the warm smile on his face, relaxed confidence exuding from him, and I nod. *He's got me alright. Hook, line, and sinker.*

The ride is actually lovely, Alexander pointing out

parts of Long Island as we fly over, and then the coast of Block Island as we approach. It feels as though we've only been in the air a few minutes, when we start descending toward to a lower altitude. I'm shocked by how quick the flight is, even though he told me it would only be around thirty minutes.

"That's ours." Alexander points out the window to a large gray structure, which seems to be made up of several buildings shaped in a large U around a pool in the backyard. It's not right on the ocean, but it's close enough that you can see it from the house.

"Where are we landing?" I half-shout into the mic attached to the headphones, noticing Alexander flinch.

"You don't have to yell, baby." He grins broadly and points to the lawn at the front of the house. "Right there."

My brow shoots up as I focus on the spot we're going to land. "Is that enough room?" I dart my gaze to him.

"More than enough." He nods, his smile still wide. I can tell already that he's lighter, less stressed. Is it leaving the city, being in a place he considers home, or is it me? I'm not really sure, but I like him like this.

My stomach flip-flops as the helicopter suddenly stops moving forward and we seem to plummet to the ground. We aren't of course, we're simply landing, but as it's my first time in a helicopter, it's a new experience for me. I feel like I'm in an elevator going down, but at a much higher rate of speed. I'm delighted at how gentle the actual landing is when we touch the ground.

Alexander swipes the headset off, so I follow suit. He

leans forward to unlatch my straps, brushing his lips across mine before he sits back. "Ready?"

I nod, the door beside me opening. The co-pilot has already freed himself and climbed out to help us exit. Once we were both off safely, he grabs our bags and hands them to Alexander. "We'll see you here on Monday, sir?"

"Yes, at five." He shakes his head. "Thanks for everything, Tom." He turns back to me. "Let's go see the house."

From the front, the house looks normal. It's a Cape style, covered in weathered, gray clapboard. The roof looks a bit worn, but I imagine between the sun, salt water, and ocean winds, all the structures on the island take a beating. We walk through a stoned patio porch to a front door, Alexander entering a code on a keypad before pushing it open.

"Welcome." He stands aside, sweeping his arm out in invitation to enter.

"Thank you." I offer him a sheepish smile as I stroll past him into the house. I gasp as I take in the view from the windows on the opposite side of the room we're in. Rays of sunshine brighten an infinity pool that overlooks a lawn so green it seems to sparkle, the ocean shimmering in the background. It's stunning.

"Wow." I twist to look at Alexander. "It's beautiful here." The entire bottom floor of the house is one big open space, all natural-colored wood floors and ceilings, decorated with comfortable white furniture everywhere. It's comfy and cozy and everything you'd expect from a home on an island.

"It's okay." He kicks the door closed with his foot, dropping our bags on the floor, his focus entirely on me as he prowls closer. "I see something more beautiful."

"Oh." I utter. His arm loops around my waist to haul me flush. "Oh!" This time it comes out on a gulp, his intentions made more obvious by his hard length pressing into my waist. I lift my head until my eyes meet his.

"We're not on university property anymore. Not in campus housing, not in class, not even in the fucking state." He proclaims, his voice low and gravelly, my legs turning to jelly.

"No more-" His mouth presses against my neck to deposit a hot kiss, "rules."

The heat of his tongue trails along my jaw until he reaches my ear. His mouth scorching as it vibrates against my skin. "I'm going to fuck you on every surface in this house."

My core throbs, lava whooshing through my veins, igniting my desire into a burning flame, hot and unquenchable. "Finally." I melt in approval, my arms folding around the back of his neck as I crush my lips to his.

His hands cup under my ass to lift me, my legs wrapping around his waist as he carries me deeper into the house. Our mouths stay fused, our tongues playing with each other. He lowers my bottom against something hard, and I pull away long enough to realize it's the dining room table.

"Lunch is served." He grins wickedly, grabbing the bottom of his shirt to rip it over his head.

"Am I lunch?" I check, clenching onto my lower lip to contain the groan wanting to escape when he exposes his chest. *He's fucking perfection.*

"Lunch. Dinner. Dessert." He pulls my sandals off my feet, one by one. Then he moves his fingers, skimming up my bare legs, under the hem of the dress I'm wearing. He doesn't stop until he's reached the band of my panties, which he grips onto before sliding them off of me.

He scrunches the white cotton in his fist, lifting it to his nose, inhaling deeply, his eyes locked on mine. "I've wanted to do this since you taunted me with these in class yesterday." He tilts his head and makes a tsking sound as he drops them beside my head. "I still haven't had the chance to punish you properly."

My heart pounds so hard I'm sure he can hear it. My core throbs in response to his words, excitement coursing through me as I play his game. "But, Professor, couldn't I do some extra homework or stay after class to clean the erasers?" I blink slowly, peering up at him under my lashes.

"Oh, I have some extra credit work you can do." He places a hand on the inside of each one of my thighs, slowly pushing until my legs part wide, his attention shifting to below my waist as he drops to his knees.

His fingers glide lower, trailing like a feather over my skin, every hair on my body standing at attention, my breath panting out of me. One finger grazes over the hood of my clit, and I let out a whimper. Alexander's eyes dart to mine as he lets out a small growl, this time dragging his digit through my folds. "I love hearing you whimper, but I'd much rather hear you scream my name."

It doesn't take long for me to grant his request as he bends forward, his tongue dragging up my center in one long, hard stroke, his name tumbling from my lips. "Yes, just like that, but louder." He chuckles, the vibration against my core delicious, erased a second later when he licks me again. "Jesus, you fucking taste amazing."

"That feels fucking amazing." I spread my legs wider. "Don't stop."

He peeks up at me, his grin feral. "Not until you come all over my face, Princess." He dives back in, keeping his promise, feasting on me like a starving man. My fingers claw at the hair on his head, my own head thrashing back and forth as I feel my body climb higher, and higher. A second later, I'm crashing to earth, every cell in my body exploding as my orgasm detonates, and I scream his name as requested.

"I need to be in you." He pants, rising to stand, yanking the button of his jeans open before shoving them down his legs. His hands grip my waist to haul my ass down to the end of the table, and in one thrust, he buries himself inside of me. "Fuck." His head falls back on his shoulders as he groans. "So goddamn tight."

His fingers dig into my hips as he slides back before plunging deep, grunting when his balls slap against me. His eyes are closed, his mouth open, his nostrils flaring as he continues to drive into me.

When he slept with me back in August, he was gentle

and kind and everything I needed him to be. Now, he was showing me his true self, and I loved it. This is what I wanted from him. I arch my back, my hands clinging to the edge of the table to hold me in place, every thrust from him a claiming.

"Oh shit." Alexander groans as he slides completely out of me, taking a step back, his chest rising and falling as he scrapes a hand through his hair. "I forgot to put a condom on."

Shit. I sit up. I didn't even realize either. "I take the shot."

"I've never forgotten to put a condom on before." He declares like he needs to convince me.

"It's okay." I try to reassure him. "I won't get pregnant."

"It's not that." He shakes his head, his eyes meeting mine. "I mean, I obviously don't want to get you pregnant. But, it's just that I've slept with too many women to count."

"Really?" My brow arches, as I sit up straighter. "This is what you think is helpful right now?"

"No, listen, I'm not done." He closes the distance between us, resting his hands on my legs. "I have never, not once, forgotten to put a condom on. Until now." His eyes lock onto mine. "Until you."

"Oh." I murmur, understanding what I think he's trying to tell me.

"You make me forget everything, Summer. You make me want to break down every barrier I've ever built. I want to feel every single thing with you."

Heat floods my body at his confession, my heart beating like a hammer hitting my ribcage. "Alexander." His name, a whisper on my lips before he leans forward, capturing them against his own. I reach between us and guide him back inside of me, his mouth falling open on a moan as he sinks deeper.

He lowers my back to the table, his fingers trailing over my covered breasts and stomach before fusing around my waist. "I'm going to fuck you so hard. Make you pay for every time you teased me. For every wet dream you made me had. For every night I lost sleep over you. For that god damn skirt you had on yesterday."

He punctuates the end of each sentence with a hard piston of his hips, his cock hard, so hard as it plunges into me, pleasure consuming me. I have a death grip on the edge of the table as I try to meet him thrust for thrust, sweat from his chest dripping onto me. I want to lick every drop off of him, feel every bump and ridge of him with my tongue. Instead, I tell him how good he feels and to not stop.

"I'm going to come, Summer." He warns, his restraint all but gone as he continues to slam inside of me.

"Yes, yes, please." I beg, wanting to feel every ounce of what he has to give.

"Fuck!" He roars, bucking into me a final time, my own orgasm crashing over me as I feel his cock pulse out his hot release.

Chapter Twenty

~Alexander~

"Are you alright?" I huff out, my body lying over hers, as I try to recover some form of sanity. My mind is fucking blown. I've never been bare in a woman, let alone come in one. It feels better than anything I've ever experienced before.

It was like sliding into silk, soft and warm, and god, she was so damn tight. I want to fuck her again and again. Although, I'm not quite sure how she feels about that at the moment. Especially after what I just did to her.

"Perfect." She murmurs under me. "Although, breathing is starting to get a bit difficult with you on top of me."

I don't want to remove my dick from the most divine place it's ever been, but hate the thought of Summer being uncomfortable even more. I push myself up, hovering over her long enough to crush her mouth to mine, then slowly slide out of heaven. I watch as my cum leaks out of her, and my cock instantly gets hard again. I've branded her as mine, with my seeds of life, something so foreign and primal to me, and also the biggest fucking turn-on.

"Stay there one second while I get something to wipe you." I hold a finger up as I shove my pants off the rest of the way, then stride to the kitchen. I find a towel in one of the drawers and bring it over to her. I wipe gently, knowing I was the exact opposite with her a few minutes ago. As if it's even possible, my dick gets harder. I glance up to find her staring as my length bobs against my navel, her lower lip stuck between her teeth again.

"I can give you something to put in that mouth if you want?" I suggest, not kidding in the least.

"How are you still hard after that?" Her cheeks flush a beautiful shade of pink as her eyes dart from my waist to my face.

"This is what you fucking do to me." I toss the towel onto the floor, then tug her upright, cupping her face with my hands. "It's what you've been doing to me for the last three months."

"Sorry?" She grins, her cheeks lifting under my palms. My attention falls to her bruise again, and I feather my thumb over it.

"Does it hurt?"

"Only when I smile." She confesses on a shrug.

"What can I do for you?" I ask, wanting to take care of her. Wanting to do anything that makes her feel better.

"You're already doing it." She tilts forward and kisses

me. It's warm and sweet, and I hum in appreciation when she pulls away. "I do have to go to the bathroom. Can you show me where it is?"

"Of course." I help her off the table, watching as she slides her panties back on, a salacious grin on my face. "I'm just going to take those off of you again."

"I hope so." She flashes me a coy smile.

"I've created a monster." I cock my head as I appraise her.

"Your worst nightmare." She jests as she follows where I lead.

"My absolute best dream." I counter, twirling around to trap her against the nearest wall, my hard length pressing into her. "And I never want to wake up."

"Alexander." She breathes my name on an exhale. I can feel her pulse racing under my grip.

"Summer." I whisper back as I stare into her wide eyes, the blue so clear I can see myself reflecting in them. Does she see what I see? Because I think I might be falling in love with her. And instead of scaring the shit out of me, it makes me feel better than I ever have. I kiss her. Softly this time, my lips feathering over hers, our breath becoming one as we fuse together.

After a moment, I pull away, dropping her hands as I move back. I take a step through the doorway of the bedroom I usually stay in. "The bathroom's right through there."

"That thing is going to be classified as a dangerous weapon." She points to my dick, still hard. Still throbbing. "It leaked onto my dress." She frowns as she glances down at the wet stain on the fabric in the middle of her stomach.

"Guess you're just going to have to take it off." I shrug, mocking disappointment.

"I see what you're doing there." She giggles, walking past me towards the bathroom. She shuts the door behind her after she enters, wanting some privacy, or maybe to make sure I don't follow her in there. Either way, I don't blame her.

I decide I should probably try and act a little less like a love-struck teenager having sex for the first time, and open one of the dresser drawers to grab a pair of shorts. I slide them on, shoving my softening dick down, then walk over to the large plate-glass windows that look out over the back lawn and the ocean beyond. It's a gorgeous day and I wonder if I should take Summer for a walk down to the beach to see how warm the water is.

"You got dressed." Her voice pulls me out of my thoughts, and I spin around, my eyes popping wide.

"You got undressed." My voice husky as I prowl in her direction.

"My dress was dirty." She shrugs, sucking her bottom lip between her teeth again. I stop in front of her, my brow furrowing when I notice the angry bruise on her side.

"I'm going to kill that mother-fucker." I growl under my breath, brushing my fingers as lightly as possible over her marred skin.

"I'm fine." She places a hand flat on my chest and shoves me back until my legs hit the bed. Then she shoves with both hands, my ass landing on the comforter.

Before I can utter a word, she climbs on top of me, straddles my waist, and grinds her core against my very hard again cock. "Didn't you say you wanted to fuck me on every surface in this house?"

"Did you just say fuck?" I ask, shocked.

"It's the monster in me." She purrs, leaning to kiss me, her pink tongue darting out to swipe against my lips before covering them.

Because I'm a man that knows how to honor his word, and play fair, I enjoy every moment of letting her fuck me on my bed. And then I return the favor, on the couch, on the kitchen counter, after we had some fruit we found in the fridge, we do it again in the bed. Where we finally fell asleep, exhaustion hitting us both.

We don't wake until early the next morning, and just to make sure I don't disappoint on my promises, I fuck her against the wall in the shower. We're back in the kitchen now, her sitting on one of the stools at the counter, watching as I scramble eggs.

"I never would have pegged you for a man that cooked." She muses, sipping on a cup of coffee I also made her. She looks stunning. She's in my blue t-shirt, her hair is messy, her cheeks are flushed, and her eyes are sparkling.

"I'm not." I assure her. "I make three things. Scrambled eggs, coffee and a really mean grilled cheese."

"Good to know." She grins. "Are you sure I can't do anything to help?"

"Nope. Just let me feed and nourish you so I can have my way with you again." I cock a grin at her, which she returns, her cheeks flushing. She is still my shy and innocent dove, even if she tries to pretend otherwise.

"Is that a hot tub out there beside the pool?" She gestures toward a round, wooden cover on the deck.

"It sure is." I confirm, pouring the eggs into the pan, a loud sizzle sounding before I start to stir them. "It should be on. I can check after."

"I might actually be able to walk again if I could soak in that for a little while."

"Wait, did you just make a joke about how much fucking we've done?" I try to contain the constant smile I've been wearing in her presence.

"No joke, mister!" Her brows shoot up as she points to her nether region. "I'm sore as hell down there!"

"I'll try and keep my hands off you for a little while." I promise, pretending to pout.

"I wasn't complaining." She mumbles around her cup as she takes another drink of her coffee. "Besides, there's other ways we can make each other happy." She flashes me a naughty grin.

I huff out loud with laughter. "It's confirmed. I've definitely created a monster."

"At least I'm your monster." She jokes.

"All mine." I look her directly in the eye, my smile gone as I realize there is no way I'll be sharing her with anyone else.

Ever.

Fuck.

I think I went and fell in love.

Chapter Twenty-One

~Summer~

It feels like I'm in a dream. A dream too perfect to be true. I keep pinching myself to make sure I'm awake. This man. He's like a different person since we've been in Block Island. Granted, it's only been twenty-four hours, but it's like a flip has been switched.

I love every single minute of this new man, but I'd be lying if I didn't say I wasn't waiting for the other shoe to drop. Or his other personality to rear its ugly head. This was very Dr. Jekyll, Mr. Hyde behavior. And while he has always been hot and cold with me, having him run at a constant hot, is entirely new.

I was washing our breakfast dishes, even though Alexander insisted I could leave them for the help. As if. There he went, trying to pretend he wasn't rich again. He was outside getting the hot tub ready for me. I watch through the window as he pushes the heavy wooden lid off and marvel once again at his physique. Have I mentioned he has abs to die for?

The hot tub is sunken into the deck, steam rising off the water now that the cover has been removed. He looks over his shoulder at the kitchen window, giving me a thumbs up when he sees me ogling him. At least I wasn't drooling. I smile and wave to him, wiping my hands on a dish towel. He ambles back across the deck, swiping a foot into the water of the pool, as he makes his way back inside.

"It doesn't feel like the pool heater is on, but the hot tub definitely is, if you want to go in." He slides the screen door closed behind him. "It's beautiful out there."

"I definitely want to go in." I toss the towel on the counter and meet him halfway across the room. He wraps me in a hug, his lips pressing against mine several times.

"Let me go put my bathing suit on."

"Or not." He murmurs against my lips through another kiss.

"I thought you were going to keep your hands off me." I giggle against his mouth.

"Doesn't mean I don't want to look." He chuckles, pulling back to grin at me.

"You are bad, Alexander Walker."

"News flash, Princess, this is not new information." He waggles his brows, then smacks me lightly on the ass. "Go. Put your suit on. Covered or naked, you still make me hard as a rock." To prove his point, he shoves his waist into mine.

"You're insatiable." I cry out in mock disbelief.

"Only for you, baby. Only for you." He plants a final kiss against my lips before pulling away. "I'm going naked. You've been warned." He shoves his shorts down his legs, steps out of them, and walks, in all his full-moon glory, back out to the hot tub.

I quickly change into the bikini I brought, frowning when I look at my reflection. The bruise on my side is an ugly blue and purple, the one on my cheek a dark red. It's a stark reminder that we're hiding out in paradise now, but sooner or later, I'm going to have to go back and face reality. I shake off my thoughts. Not happening today. Today I want to enjoy the time I have with Alexander.

I stride back through the kitchen, stopping when I notice the wine fridge tucked into the lower cabinet of the island. I pull out a bottle, snatch two glasses off a nearby rack, and head outside.

"I brought refreshments." I sing-song, waving the bottle in front of me.

"Princess, it's nine-thirty in the morning and you're already trying to get me drunk?" He chuckles, rising from the tub as I approach, his body a dripping, glistening specimen of perfection. He's hard, again, and I suck my lower lip between my teeth, distracting from the groan I want to send out to the universe.

"It's perfectly acceptable to have mimosas on Sunday for brunch." I assure him, setting the bottle and glasses down beside the hot tub, before stepping in beside him.

"Except you forgot the orange juice and that's a two-hundred-dollar bottle of Dom." He drawls, yanking me flush, his wet lips nipping mine.

"Semantics." I giggle, pushing away from him before things progress. "Open it?" I tilt my head to the champagne.

"At your service, Princess." He gives a playful bow, then pops the cork, both of us letting out a little yelp of joy at the sound. He pours us both a glass, then moves to sit beside me as he hands me one.

I take a sip, the bubbles tickling my nose as I do, humming at the yumminess. "So good."

"I agree." He takes a gulp, a wide smile breaking across his face as he shakes his head.

"What?" I wonder out loud.

"This is so not how I pictured my weekend when you forced me out of my own classroom on Friday." He chuffs. "Not that I'm complaining." He leans over and brushes a kiss against my battered cheek.

"Uh, yeah, me either." I wanted to get him to admit that he had feelings for me, but this was entirely more than I could have hoped for.

"I have a question for you." He skims his fingers over the water, a nervous tilt to his voice.

"Okay…"

"Did you fuck Davenport?" He narrows his gaze on me, crinkles forming on the outside edges of his eyes.

I choke on the sip of champagne currently half way down my throat, anger slashing through me. "What?" I splutter when I'm done coughing.

"He seemed pretty damn friendly with you on Tuesday." His eyes still dark with jealousy.

"Not that it's any of your business, but no." I take a gulp from my flute, fire burning in my belly. "Unlike you, I don't sleep with every person I go out with."

"So, you admit that you went out with him?" He continues to pepper questions at me.

"We met for drinks. With my cousin. And her friend Lily, who's also in your class by the way. Are you going to ask if I fucked her too?" I seethe, my nostrils flaring.

"That would at least be far better to imagine." One side of his mouth cocks up, his eyes softening. "I'm sorry. I had to know. It's been bugging the shit out of me." He rakes his wet fingers through his hair, droplets of water clinging to the dark ends. "He bugs the shit out of me."

"You have nothing to worry about." I stand, water slushing down my body, then swing a leg over him, settling myself in his lap. I wrap my hands around his neck, my glass dangling from my fingers. "You are the only one I want. The only one I think about. The only one I want to be with. The only one." I press my damp lips to his to drive my point home.

"You've turned me into a jealous simp." He mumbles against my mouth, deepening our kiss, swiping his tongue against the seam of my lips, urging me to open. Without hesitation I comply, his cock jerking underneath me to press against the material of my bathing suit.

"You're making it very hard to keep my promise right now." He pants, smoothing a hand over my cheek, his forehead leaning against mine.

"Promises were made to be broken." I purr, spearing a hand in the water to tug the tie holding my bottoms on undone. "Oops." I place a hand over my mouth as I feign innocence.

His brow shoots up, a devilish smile lifting his cheeks, his eyes sparkling with mischief, his fingers grasping the bow at the back of my neck before yanking it loose. "Double oops."

He tilts his head, his tone serious now. "Are you sure?"

I reach into the water, lift my hips, and wrench my bottom out from under me, tossing it onto the deck. "One hundred thousand percent." I rock my core against his hard length in case he needs further convincing.

He doesn't. His mouth crashes back to mine, his cock sliding into me a moment later. I hiss as he pushes me down, but it's a pain so welcome, my center pulses around him. Once I'm seated firmly on him, I grind my hips back and forth, water sloshing over the rim of the tub, knocking both our glasses over. I reach for them, but he shakes his head, his dark eyes locked on me.

"Don't you dare stop." He growls. "You want more champagne?" He doesn't bother waiting for a reply, instead grabbing the bottle by the hilt, holding it over my mouth. "Open." He instructs.

I lean my head back, widening my jaw, the cool bubbly liquid pouring in a second later. I swallow, but it begins pouring over my chin. He adjusts the stream so it's flooding over my chest, my breasts peaking from the hot contrast of the tub water.

A low groan rumbles from him as he discards the bottle behind him. "You are so fucking sexy." He bends and sucks hard onto my nipple, biting with his teeth, then soothing with his tongue.

My body has a mind of its own, my legs locked tight against his thighs as I drive myself up and down his cock like I'm a jockey in the Kentucky Derby. Unintelligible words leave me with each exhale, my arms locked around Alexander's neck for leverage.

"Hold on." He rises suddenly, water whooshing in all directions as he steps onto the deck, turning to lay me on my back. My ankles clamp around his waist, our bodies staying fused.

"Need more." He growls into my ear, the vibration sparking a lightning bolt of tingles on every surface of my body.

"More." I echo, more than ready for whatever he has to give. He doesn't hesitate, burying himself to the hilt, ramming into me again and again until we both tumble into ecstasy, screaming out to the heavens.

Chapter Twenty-Two

~Alexander~

I stare at her naked perfection, lounging beside me on the pool chaise, and wonder for the twentieth time this weekend how the hell I got here. Not in a million years did I see myself falling for anyone, let alone someone like her. She was too good for me. But I didn't care. I wanted her anyway and had to figure out how I was going to make that happen. Her being my student was a complication I didn't know how to solve.

And she was so young. Almost a decade younger than me. Was it wrong for me to want to claim her as mine when she still had so much youth, so much living she hadn't even begun to experience yet? But I could share all that with her, couldn't I?

"I can feel you leering at me." She mumbles, the corner of her mouth tugging up.

"You're a vision. Not looking is impossible." I confirm.

"Don't go falling for me, Professor." She turns her head, pulling the sunglasses down her nose to peer at me over the rim. "That's asking for trouble neither of us wants."

"Might be too late." I confess, shocking myself as the words fall freely without thought.

She bolts to a sitting position, whipping her glasses off to reveal wide, saucer like eyes, the blue so bright in the sun. "What?"

I pull myself up, turning my body so I'm facing her, my legs intertwining with hers. I place a hand over her knee, my thumb stroking her warm skin in a lazy circle. "You heard me."

"But…" Her voice trails off as she continues to stare at me, apparently lost for words for once.

"I know." I swipe my own sunglasses off, pinching the bridge of my nose on an exhale.

"You said you don't do relationships." She utters, her brow drawn together.

"I don't." I profess, then shrug. "Or, at least, I've never wanted to." I tighten my fingers around her knee. "Until now."

"Alex." Her breath catches in her throat, as she shakes her head. "I'm not sure what I'm supposed to say."

"Say you want the same thing." I urge, scooting closer to her, my hand sliding up her bare thigh.

Her head tilts as she examines me. "What about the real world? I'm your student. We can't do this." She waves her hand between us. "At least, not in the city or at the university."

"But is it what you want?" I press her for more. "Would you keep seeing me if you could?"

Her gaze is penetrating as she continues to analyze me, my heart racing at her hesitation, the next words blurting out of me, again without any forethought. "I'm falling for you, Summer. I'm not sure I can imagine my days without you in them now. You've burrowed under my skin, into my every thought, into my heart."

"This feels too good to be true." She challenges, sliding her hand over mine, lacing our fingers together. "And you know what they say about things that seem too good to be true." She shrugs, sadness tinging her voice. "I'm so afraid it's going to end badly."

"You don't think this scares the hell out of me?" I confess. "Summer, I have never brought a woman to my family's home, to my apartment in the city." My tone darkening. "Fucked someone bare, again and again and wanted more." I shake my head. "This is different. You're different."

"I want to say yes, so badly, Alexander." She blinks, so much hope shining in her reflection.

"Then say yes." I implore, leaning forward, snaking my hand around the back of her neck to bring her forehead to mine.

"Please don't break my heart." She whispers. "I don't know if I could survive it."

"Don't break mine." I counter, sealing our fears with a

kiss, then leaning back. "I want this. You. More than anything, Summer."

"You're going to make me fall in love with you." She warns me, pinning me with her gaze.

"I'll be here, ready to catch you." I promise, kissing her again. I want nothing more than to scoop her up and carry her to my bed like a caveman, but know I need to give her body a break, so suggest an alternative. "Let's go take showers. We can walk down the beach to a great restaurant I know."

"That sounds wonderful." Her smile radiant. "I'm starving."

A few hours later, we stroll down the beach, hand in hand. She looks radiant in a dress the color of sunshine, a straw hat on her head, her lips coated in a pink gloss. Sandals dangle from her other hand as her feet amble over the wet sand, the waves lapping over her toes every now and then.

"Are you happy?" I wonder out loud, tugging her to me as I absorb every facet of her.

"Deliriously." A wide grin gracing her face as she beams up at me. "Are you?"

"Dangerously so." I acquiesce on a chuckle, stealing a kiss. "It's a foreign concept to me."

We continue walking down the beach, the restaurant looming in the horizon now.

"How so?" She coaxes for more.

I exhale, not sure how to explain but give it a try. "I've known pleasure. Felt moments of happiness." I cock a wry look her way. "Usually when I was buried in someone."

"Alexander!" She swats my arm. "Gross. And also, TMI."

"But see, that's what I'm trying to convey." I frown, struggling with my new found feelings. "It's going to sound like such a fucking cliché when I say it out loud."

"Just say it." She demands. "I promise I won't poke fun."

"You are every god damn thing I never knew I wanted. Or needed." I blow out a long breath trying to quell my nerves as I complete my thought. "I've never felt more complete."

Her feet stutter to a halt, her body twisting to face mine, out hands still locked together, her mouth parted slightly as she tries to say something, but I interrupt. "I think what I'm trying to say, and not very well, is I've fallen in love you."

"You're in love with me?" She breathes out her question, her teeth capturing her lower lip a second later as she begins chewing it to a pulp, her brow furrowing.

"Don't do that." I use my thumb to tug her lip free. I bend, darting the tip of my tongue out to sweep over the now tender flesh. "I love you." I murmur against her mouth, then seal my profession, crushing my mouth over hers in a deep kiss.

I pull back, searching her face for some kind of response, her wide eyes locking with mine. "I think this is the first time I've rendered you speechless." My heart is thundering against my ribs, anxiety causing my pulse to race as I worry I declared my feelings too soon.

"I didn't dare to hope." She finally replies, her voice a whisper, barely heard over the waves lapping against the shore. She blinks rapidly, trying to keep the tears brimming in her eyes at bay. "I never thought it was possible, so I shoved my feelings so deep, trying to fool myself into believing I could keep things simple with you." She shakes her head, a tear breaking free to slide down her cheek. "But I think I've been in love with you from the moment we met." A soft giggle escaping as she smiles shyly. "How's that for a cliché?"

"Say it again." I demand, needing to hear it again.

"I love you, Alexander." She shrugs, her cheeks lifting higher. "Sorry, not sorry."

Our bodies melt together as we claim each other with a heated kiss, her fingers tangling in my hair, my arms locking her to me. I groan, regret invading every pore at the realization I can't sate the need throbbing below my waist. To truly claim her, to scream out loud that she's mine, and mine alone.

I tear myself off her after a moment, panting, sporting a smile bright enough to light up night. "Come on." I yank her to my side, sliding an arm around her waist. "Let's go get drunk."

Fifteen minutes later, we slush through the dry sand, and weave through the outside table at Ballard's to the hostess stand. Steve, the owner, notices me, and strolls over, offering a wave. "Alex!" He shakes my hand, clapping my shoulder with the other. "Are you here with the family for the weekend?"

"My girlfriend." I state, saying the words out loud a shock to my ears, nodding towards her. "This is Summer."

"Beautiful name for my favorite season." He offers her his hand, which she takes. "Wonderful to meet you, Summer. I'm Steve."

He focuses his attention back to me. "You want a table for dinner?" He snags two menus from the stand next to him, and I nod. "Inside or out?"

I arch a brow at Summer to gage her preference. "Definitely outside." She replies. "It's too nice a night not to enjoy it."

"It's the full moon." We follow as Steve starts leading us to an available table. "We're having a bonfire tonight as well, starting at eight-thirty, if you want to join us later."

"Thanks." I help Summer into her chair, then sit beside her, both of us facing the ocean. "We just might take you up on that."

"I'll send Jenny right over to take your drink orders." He winks, dropping a quick pat on my shoulder as he departs. "Enjoy."

We order margaritas and a bowl of steamers to start, our fingers locked together between us on the table.

"I don't want to ruin this perfect night, but what are we going to do when we go home tomorrow?" She probes, concern in her voice.

"Let's worry about that tomorrow." I suggest. "We'll

figure out how to make this work." I lie through my teeth, because I know, even though I don't want to admit it, the real world is a bitch.

Chapter Twenty-Three

~Summer~

"Stop being so loud." I demand, shoving my head under the covers. How many damn margaritas did I have last night, because it feels like a sledge hammer is pounding my skull from the inside out.

"It's after eleven, Princess." Alexander's deep voice advises from above, his hands falling on each side of me, the heat from his body covering me. "And all I did was say good morning." His chest vibrates against my back when he chuckles.

"How are you so chipper?" I grumble, wondering what I'm being punished for. No one deserves to feel this bad in the morning, no matter how many shots of tequila they may or may not have done.

"I've already gone for a run, and swam fifty laps." He

plants a kiss against the back of my hair. "Exercise is the best cure for any hangover."

"I hate you." I roll onto my side, curling myself into a tight ball, his body aligning to wrap around me.

"No you don't." He reminds me. "You love me." His arms clench tighter. "At least, that's what you kept yelling out on more than one occasion last night." His chest vibrates again.

I toss the blanket off my head, twisting to look at him. "We had sex last night?"

"Several times." His brow furrows. "You don't remember?" He frowns. "On the beach, and then in the shower because we were both covered in sand."

"Oh my god." I slap a hand over my face, which I'm sure is red with mortification. "Please tell me I didn't make a complete fool of myself."

"You were amazing." He assures me. "But now I feel like a complete ass for not realizing just how drunk you were. I wouldn't have taken advantage of you."

"Oh, something tells me I probably wasn't complaining." I mutter, sliding my fingers away to bury my head in my pillow. "I'm so sorry." It comes out all muffled, but I'm too humiliated to lift my head and repeat myself.

"No, I'm sorry." He insists, his tone firm. "It's my job to protect and take care of you. I should have known you were too drunk."

I roll over, wiggling my body until I can meet him in the eye. "You were drunk too. You didn't do anything wrong."

"I'm almost ten years older than you. I should fucking

know better." He continues to argue his point, but I press a finger to his lips.

"Stop." I roll my eyes. "Just tell me I had a good time."

"There is no doubt that you enjoyed every second." His lips cock up, a single brow arching high. "I'd be happy to provide a replay, if you think it would jog your memory."

I shake my head. "Not unless you're into vomit, because I think that's where I'm headed." I jump out of the bed, slamming my hand over my mouth as I race to the toilet. I make it just in time, the contents of my stomach retching from me.

I feel my hair being bunched into a ball behind my neck, and try to slap him away, but end up needing my hands to brace myself as more of my guts spill out of me. I want to die. From embarrassment, and because I feel so utterly awful.

"I've got you." His hand rubs small, gentle circles against my back as he continues to hold my hair. I rest my bottom on my knees, dropping my head against the crook of my arm, praying the worst is over. I'm never drinking again.

"Can I get you anything?" He asks softly.

"My dignity?" I choke out, moaning as a cramp seizes my stomach.

"Your dignity is firmly intact. Still the apple of my eye." He assures me as his palm continues to soothe me.

"Still love me?" I check, lifting my head to peek over my shoulder at him.

"More than ever." He bends, depositing a kiss against my neck. "Think you're done?"

"I think so." I nod, attempting to stand, his arm sliding around my waist to assist me.

"Let's get you back in bed for a little while. I'll get you some ginger ale and crackers." I collapse back on the bed, the covers draping over me a second later as he tucks me in. "Do you think you can handle Advil?"

"Let's start with the soda and go from there." I plop my arm across my eyes to block out the light.

"You got it."

"Baby?" I blink awake to the warmth of fingers brushing strands of hair off my cheek. "How are you?"

I yawn, belatedly covering my mouth as I realize my breath must be horrid. "Sorry." I grimace, recalling my puking event from earlier. I attempt to yank the covers back over my head trying to hide. I have never felt more my age than this moment.

Alexander tears the blankets out of my grasp, his deep, blue eyes soft as he stares down at me. "You don't have to hide from me." He presses a kiss to my forehead. "Nothing you do will ever change the way I feel about you."

"Ugh." I groan. "Why do you have to be so perfect?"

"Trust me, I'm far from perfect." He scoffs. "You give

me way more credit than I deserve. You'll come to see that the more time you spend with me."

"I'll believe that when I see it." I mumble, noticing the sun is low in the sky. "What time is it?"

"Almost three-thirty." He strokes his palm lovingly over my cheek. "I wanted to let you rest as long as possible, but thinking you may want a shower before the helicopter arrives."

"I wasted an entire day." I frown. "Time we could have been spending together." I push myself to sit up beside him. "I'm sorry, Alex."

"You called me Alex." He muses, tilting his head.

"Is that okay?"

"I like it." He smiles, his eyes lighting up. "I was more concerned with how you were feeling."

"I think I feel better." I swing my legs off the bed and stand. "Thank you taking care of me. For letting me sleep."

"Of course. Are you hungry? I can make you something while you shower?" As if on cue, my stomach grumbles loudly, both of us laughing out loud.

"I think that's a yes." I grin, rubbing my center.

"Eggs or grilled cheese?" He offers the only two options he knows he can make.

"Definitely grilled cheese."

Twenty minutes later, freshly showered, teeth brushed, and fresh clothes, I'm sitting in the kitchen, sinking my teeth into the tastiest sandwich I've ever eaten. "What in the world did you put in this? It's delicious!"

"If I tell you, I'll have to kill you." He states,

completely serious. "It's a family recipe, and we've all been sworn to secrecy."

"Well, you could serve these in a restaurant and make a killing." I take another bite, moaning at the cheesiness melting in my mouth.

"Our ride will be here soon." He reminds me, one corner of his mouth turning down. "We need to talk about how to handle things back in the city."

"Can't we just hide out here forever?" I plead, only half kidding.

"You have no idea how tempting that idea is to me." He places his elbows on the counter, leaning closer to me. "Because everything will be different the minute we land."

I stop chewing, my gaze penetrating his as I try to figure out what he's thinking. "Okay…"

"I think it would be better if I dropped you at your aunt and uncle's apartment. Coming back to mine might be pushing our luck further than we already have, and your locks aren't getting changed until tomorrow." He straightens and begins pacing. "We'll need to stay apart and minimize our contact anywhere on University property, including in my classroom. I'm going to ask Tim to grade all of your work going forward so there's no concern of favoritism in your grade."

I straighten in my chair, crossing my arms, my pulse starting to race. "How exactly are we going to have any kind of a relationship with these rules?"

He mimics my posture, crossing his arms as his stance widens. "We don't."

"Wha—" I start, interrupted when he speaks over me.

"Not until the semester is over, and you aren't in my class anymore." He lifts his shoulders, shaking his head. "It's the only way."

I huff out a breath, narrowing my eyes as I peer over at him. "It's not the only way."

"What else would you suggest, Summer? Because seeing each other puts you at risk, and I don't want that for you. I could care less what happens to me."

"So, I don't get any say in this decision at all? You've just decided we're going to wait almost two months, and not see each other?" I throw my hands in the air, my cheeks heating as my voice rises.

"It's seven weeks." He iterates. "We can text, talk on the phone. And there are weekends. We can make plans to meet and spend time together then."

I shake my head, breaking his gaze to stare down at the counter. "This feels wrong. And us being together shouldn't be wrong."

He strides to me, putting a finger under my chin lifting it until our eyes meet. "We are not wrong. Nothing has ever felt more right." He sweeps a kiss over my mouth. "I'm already in agony when I think about not being able to touch you, hold you, make love to you. Especially when you'll be twenty-five feet in front of me in my class-room." He draws me into a hug, pulling me close, his lips murmuring against my ear. "But I can do anything for seven weeks if it leads to forever with you."

"Alex." I whisper, turning my face to his. "Forever?"

"I'm in love with you, Summer."

The weight of his words sink in, the intensity of his gaze even heavier. This man loves me. I can see it in every single action, feel it in every touch, hear it in the plea of his voice. How is this real? He is undeniably perfect, and if I can't commit to seven weeks, I don't deserve him. He's right, seven weeks is nothing in the big picture.

"I love you too, Alex."

Chapter Twenty~Four

~Alexander~

The flight back is quiet. Too quiet. She always has something to say, even if it's not good. Her silence worries me. This whole situation worries me. But I'm not sure what other choice we have. I will not comprise her or her well-being so we can go public with our relationship. Not when in just seven weeks it won't be an issue.

"You okay?" My hand clasps tighter onto hers. I want all the contact I can get with her while I still can.

She nods, gracing me with a small smile. But still, it's more silence. I wish I knew what was going through her head. Usually she doesn't have a filter, so I never have to wonder. This is going to be the longest seven weeks of my life.

We land, a car waiting when we do. I transfer our

bags, and ride with her to her aunt and uncle's apartment. My body is pressed against hers in the back seat, my arm snaked over her shoulder, her head resting on mine.

"I'm fine, Alex." It's like she can read my mind. "I'll see you in class tomorrow, and I'll call you once I'm settled at my aunt's."

"I know." I press a kiss to the side of her cheek. "But I miss you already."

"Try not to look too sexy in class tomorrow." She jokes, smiling over at me. "Although, you'd look good in a damn paper bag."

"Look who's talking." I chuff out a retort. "No repeats of what you wore on Friday to class or I'll be throwing you over my desk and all bets will be off."

"I promise." She sighs in agreement as we pull up to the address she gave. It's on Fifth Ave, across the street from Central Park. These people had more money than God. There's a doorman standing outside the entrance, so I feel comfortable that she'll be more than safe here.

"You'll call me?" I cup her cheek.

"As soon as I'm settled." She nods under my palm.

I kiss her. It's soft and tender and the opposite of everything I want to do. Which is ravage her. "I love you."

She brushes her lips against mine one more time, before stepping out of the car. "I love you too."

The phone rings, and I roll over, snatching it off my nightstand, certain it has to be Summer. We spoke for an hour last night, but we don't have class together until ten, so I'm guessing she wants to say good morning.

"Good morning." My voice gravely, not fully awake yet.

"Good morning, Professor Walker." A male voice on the other line, and not what or who I was expecting at all. "It's Robert Johnson."

"Bob." Fuck, what the hell was the vice president of the math department calling me for on the Tuesday morning after a holiday weekend. "How can I help you?"

"I'm afraid I'm going to need you to come down to my office." The voice clears on the other end of the line before continuing. "I've already reached out to Tim to manage your class schedule this morning. Ten works for me."

"Can you tell me what this is regarding?" I inquire, certain no one could possibly have any knowledge of my relationship with Summer so quickly.

"I'm afraid it requires a face to face." He releases a heavy sigh. "It's not good though, Alexander."

"Not helping my blood pressure at all, Bob." I respond, confusion swirling in my brain.

"I'll see you at ten. My office." The line clicks, followed by silence. I stare at the phone, dumbfounded.

I make the decision not to call Summer. She's dealt with enough this weekend, and I don't want to alarm her if this matter has nothing to do with her. Although, I can't for the life of me think of what else it could be. I haven't worked as an escort in over four months, so if it was related to that, I would think it would have caught up to me long ago.

I shower, shave, dress in a suit, then choke down a coffee through my nerves. I grab an Uber to the V.P.'s office, announcing my arrival to his secretary upon entering his office. It doesn't take more than a few minutes before the door opens, Bob beckoning me inside.

"How are you, Alex?" He motions for me to take a seat.

"I'd be better if I knew what this impromptu meeting was about." I sit, unbuttoning my jacket as I do.

"Yes, let's skip the formalities and get right to it, shall we?" He frowns, spinning his computer monitor so I can see it.

My heart stops beating as my breath catches in my throat. Images of Summer and myself; naked in the hot tub, fucking on the deck, dancing arm in arm at Ballard's restaurant, us doing shots of tequila, us having sex on the beach.

"I'm sorry, Alex." His tone somber, dragging my attention from the screen to him.

"Who sent these to you?" I demand, my pulse thrumming in pace to my racing heart.

"That's what your concerned about?" Bob shakes his head, his fingers drumming against the hard wood of his desk. "They were sent anonymously. Not that it matters, Alex. The damage is done."

My attention drifts back to the grainy images on the screen. Someone had been spying on us the entire weekend. My skin crawled, the hair on the nape of my neck rising as I drag a hand through my hair. Some sick mother fucker was watching us.

"The sender was kind enough to inform us that the person in these images with you is a student of yours, Summer Knight." The sarcasm in his tone isn't missed by me. I know he's not getting any pleasure from this conversation.

"A twenty-three-year-old, consenting adult." I grind out. "But yes, she's in my physic's class."

"Alex, you know better." He steeples in fingers, his brow lined with crinkles as he stares across the desk at me. "And you know the policy regarding professors dating students." He sighs warily. "I met with President Anders earlier this morning, and because this is your first offense, neither one of us feels terminating you is necessary."

Hope blooms in my chest, but is quickly extinguished with his next statement. "You have to agree to no longer see this student, take a seminar on sexual conduct, and you'll be on probation for the next two semesters."

"And what about Ms. Knight?" It didn't matter what the answer was because it would be a cold day in hell before I ended my relationship with her.

"She will be expelled from the class, and assigned a failing grade. She will also—"

"No." I bark out my protest. "I'll resign, effective immediately. This was my mistake. She shouldn't be held responsible."

"Alex, you don't get to dictate the terms of punishment for your crimes."

"Not mine." I state angrily. "Hers." I rise, sliding my hands in my trouser pockets. "Do you know who her family is?"

Bob shakes his head. "I haven't gotten that far yet."

"She's an Erickson." I cock a brow. "Erickson Energy. She's fucking royalty. You do not want to mess with her."

Bob blows out a long sigh, his shoulders slumping. "You couldn't go and screw around with a basic co-ed. Had to pick the richest one."

I ignore his dig and continue with my original negotiation. "Put her on warning if you want, but don't fuck her future up because I couldn't keep my dick in my pants. I'll resign, leave quietly. No one will be the wiser and no further damage is done."

"You're willing to throw everything away for this girl?" Bob scratches his chin as he considers my offer.

"She's worth it." I admit with a nod.

"I'll expect your resignation by the end of the day." He shakes his head. "Against my better judgement."

"And Ms. Knight?" I press, needing to know she won't get burned by this in any way.

"She'll get a written warning, nothing more."

"Thank you, Bob." I stretch my hand out before him.

He slides his into mine, grimacing as he reluctantly shakes it. "For effectively firing you?"

"For my freedom." I explain.

"I don't understand." He releases my grip.

"You don't have to." I toss him a wave, then stride to

the door. "You'll have my resignation by the end of the day." I pause, turning back. "Do I have permission to clean my office out?"

"Just do it after hours." He frowns. "That reminds me. You have thirty days to vacate the university apartment."

"No problem." I reply, knowing I'll be out in less than a week.

"Good luck, Alex."

"I'm already the luckiest bastard on the planet." I shoot back, unable to contain the grin bursting across my face.

Chapter Twenty-Five

I'm nervous walking into class, hoping I can be in the same room with Alex for ninety minutes without making it obvious we spent the weekend in each other's arms. My steps falter when I spy Blake at our table, Lily sitting in my seat, their heads close together engrossed in a conversation.

I had completely forgotten about Blake. Nothing had happened between us last weekend when he joined Serena and I for drinks. In fact, Serena had actually seemed smitten with him, asking me a hundred questions about him since that night. She knew I was ga-ga for Alex, and wouldn't mind in the least if she threw her hat in the ring where Blake was concerned.

I had spilled all the tea to her last night about the incredible weekend I had with Alex, the sex, sex and more sex, and of course, that he told me he loved me. She was happy for me, but also worried. She wanted to know if he was still working at Temptations, and how I felt about the fact he was an escort. I think she went into temporary shock when I explained how he had stopped working there after his first date with me in June. At least, she was silent for more than three minutes, and that's a record for her.

I feel strangely light without my laptop. I brought a notebook in case I need it, intending to try and replace my computer later today. Both heads turn and snap to me as I approach.

"Hey guys." I smile and wiggle my fingers in a greeting. "What's up?"

"What happened to your cheek?" Blake's brow draws together, concern in his voice.

"Oh." I cover my bruise with my hand, almost having forgotten about it. "I was mugged Friday night."

"Mugged?" He repeats, shock evident on his features. "Where? What happened?"

"I was stupid." I attempt to wave away his worry. "I went down an alley near my building when I was leaving the library. I should have known better. But they stole my bag. I lost my laptop, my ID and my keys."

"They hit you?" This time it's Lily asking the question.

I nod, frowning. "Kicked me in the ribs for good measure too."

"Guess you won't be going down any more dark alleys again, huh?" Lily jokes, although no one laughs.

"Uh, yeah, probably not." I stammer, then change the subject. "So, what were you two whispering about?"

"You haven't heard?" Lily taunts, sneering with a shake of her head.

"No…" I place my elbows on the table to lean closer to them. "Tell me."

"Professor Walker got fired." She gloats, like it's the best news in the world. The world that just completely tilted on its axis as I digest her news.

"What?" I brace the edge of the table to hold myself steady. "Why? How do you know this?"

"Tim told me this morning." She states like it should be the most obvious thing in the world.

"Tim, the professor's assistant?" I clarify.

"Yep." She smacks her lips together on the 'p'.

"Why would he tell you?" I blurt out, still not believing what she's sharing with us.

She rolls her eyes, snorting. "Because I'm sleeping with him, and happened to be in his bed this morning when Vice President Johnson called and asked him to take over the professor's classes."

My mouth hangs wide, my stomach clenching in fear at her proclamation.

"Tim said something about an inappropriate relationship." Lily stares at me, a glint of something I can't put my finger on lurking under the surface. Is she referring to his job as an escort? She's alluded to it in the past, and we all joked about it during my aunt and uncle's party over the summer.

I needed to call Alex. I grab my phone out of my back

pocket noting he hasn't called or texted this morning. I rub my stomach and make a sour face.

"I'm actually not feeling that great. I think I'm going to skip class if the professor isn't going to be here."

Lily's brow shoots up. "You know he's not going to be back, right? He was *fired*."

"Yeah, I heard you the first time, Lily." I scowl, trying to figure out what her game is.

"Uh-huh." She murmurs, her eyes narrowing as she watches me walk away.

"I'll see you guys later." I call over my shoulder, my head spinning over Lily's news. As soon as I'm outside, I hit Alex's number. Of course, it goes straight to voicemail. I send a text asking him to call me as soon as possible.

The locksmith was supposed to change my locks this morning, so I decide to go to my building to see if it's been done. Even though it's only been a few days, not having my things, or being in my own space has been disorienting.

Finally, luck is on my side, and the locksmith is just finishing up when I arrive. The building manager is with him, and hands over my new keys. I thank them and then enter my room, bolting the new lock behind me, finally feeling some sense of peace.

I try calling Alex again, but still don't get an answer. I'm about to plug my phone in to the charger when it dings in my hand. Relief floods over me, expecting it to be Alex, disappointment washing over me when I see it's a text from a number I don't recognize.

I swipe the message, my knees turning to jelly as I

collapse onto the bed, tingles zinging over every surface of my skin as I absorb what I'm seeing.

"Summer (Knight that is) comes (again and again) for Professor Alexander Walker"

There are over a dozen pictures of us from the weekend, all of them of us having sex. My stomach rolls with nausea, my body flushing red hot as wheezing breaths puff out of me, tears begin to fall in a steady stream down my face. Who would do this to us? Before I can form another thought, my phone rings.

I gasp in relief when it's Alexander's name. I swipe to answer, stuttering a hello between gulps. "Summer?" Concern evident in his voice. "What's wrong?"

I shake my head, trying to form any words an impossible task. "I--, pictures--, text—"

"Where are you, baby?" His voice soothing. "Tell me where you are so I can come to you."

"My room." I manage between sobs.

"I'm coming." He barks into the phone. "Ten minutes. Hold on for ten minutes."

I can't stop scrolling through the photos. There are over a dozen. Someone was watching us? All weekend? Panic seizes me as I wonder if these were sent to anyone else. I can't seem to catch my breath between my heart racing and my crying.

I jump as a fist pounds against my door. "Summer, it's me!" Alex shouts from the other side. I run to the door, yanking it open after I unlock it.

I'm in his arms a second later, cocooned in his warmth, in the stead-fast safety of him. He holds me, easing us into my room, shutting the door with a kick of his foot, calming me with kind words until my sobbing subsides.

"Look." I shove my phone at him, my body still trembling.

"I've seen them, baby." He takes my phone and sets it on the table.

"What?" I exclaim, a new wave of anxiety striking. "Did you get the text as well?"

"No." He guides me to the bed, wrapping an arm around me as we sit. "Someone sent them to the head of my department." He gives a slight shake of his head. "Anonymously of course."

I twist to face him, a hiccup escaping through my nerves. "I heard you got fired."

"Actually, I resigned." He clarifies. "But news sure travels fast."

"Wait, you resigned?" My hands reach for his. "Alex…"

"It's fine." He assures me. "I'll fill you in more on that later." He brushes a kiss to my forehead. "Let's just worry about you right now."

"What are we going to do?" I inhale a deep breath trying to steady my voice.

"I've already got a team on it." His fingers brush the loose tears still falling over my cheeks. "What I'm trying to figure out is how anyone could have even known we were in Block Island. Did you tell anyone?"

I sniffle, dragging my knuckles across the bottom of my nose. "I mean, I sent a text to Serena Saturday morning. I told her about the mugging and that you were going to take me to Block Island for the weekend." I swing my gaze up to his. "But Alex, she wouldn't do this!"

"But could she have told anyone else?" He wonders out loud.

The thought hits me like a lightning bolt. The one person who seemed entirely too smug and not surprised at all over Alex's firing. "Lily." I hiss out.

"Who?" Alex's brow furrows.

"Lily. She's in your physic's class. And she's friends with Serena." I purse my lips, my mind racing as I recall each conversation we've had. Her obsession with Alex and his job at Temptations.

"Call Serena." He grabs my phone and hands it to me. "Ask her if she told anyone."

I do as he requests, my stomach plummeting when she admits she had drinks with Lily on Friday night. When I tell her what's happening, more than a few expletives spew from her. "She kept bragging about how she was sleeping with Tim, and how the professor was next on her hit list." She lets out a gasp. "This is all my fault, Summer. I got so angry when she claimed she was going to add him to her body count, I blurted out that she had no chance because he was seeing you." She lets out a huff of distress. "I am so sorry! I had no idea she would ever do anything like this."

"I know, Serena." My lips turn down as I stare across at Alex, who's listening to our conversation silently. "You couldn't have known."

"What can I do to fix this? I need to do something. Besides kick her ass of course." She declares angrily.

"Nothing right now." I sigh, my mind reeling with all the information it's trying to process. "I need to talk to Alex and figure things out. I'll call you later?"

"Please. Let me know if you need anything." She pleads, offering another apology as we hang up.

"I'm sorry, Alex." New tears springing to my eyes as I realize this is all my fault. If I hadn't shared our secret with Serena, none of this would be happening.

"Don't you dare apologize." He cups my cheeks, peppering kisses against my nose and then my lips. "This is not your fault."

My phone dings alerting me of a new mail message, and my stomach plummets in fear. I open my email, scan the new message and turn my phone to Alex. "It's from the dean. They want to see me at two today."

"You'll be fine." His lips purse in a tight line. "You'll be getting a written warning and nothing more."

My brow scrunches. "How do you know that?"

"Because it was part of the deal I made with them. I resign, and will leave quietly, as long as you are allowed to continue with your classes without any further punishment."

"No!" I jump to my feet. "I am not going to let you ruin your career for me!"

"I'm resigning." He rises to stand next to me, wrapping a hand around the back of my neck as he captures my gaze. "No mark against my record. I can go work anywhere else I want." His head falls back on his shoulders as he exhales, then looks at me again. "Honestly, I'm so fucking bored with teaching. This gives me an opportunity to decide if I want to work at my family's company, or travel, or just hang out and be your boy toy." One side of his mouth cocks up in a sexy grin.

"You don't have to do this for me." I breathe out, stepping into his body, hugging my arms around his chest.

"I'm not." He plants a kiss on the top of my head. "It's for me, and probably long overdue." He tilts his head to look me in the eye. "But Summer, just to be clear, I would set the world on fire for you."

"It kind of feels like it's already burning." I murmur, shrugging my shoulders.

"Nah." He grins. "This is nothing but a little hot spot." He gives me a quick peck. "Do you know the best part of all?"

"There's something good in this?" I marvel at his optimism.

"I'm not your professor anymore." His cheeks lift as he flashes me a broad smile.

"Oh." I exclaim as he lowers me to the bed, realization dawning.

"No more rules." He declares, spending the next thirty minutes enjoying his new found freedom.

Chapter Twenty~Six

It's two months later, and to say life couldn't be any better would be an understatement. The first few weeks after I resigned were really rough for Summer. Although none of our pictures were leaked to any other source, rumors about my resignation ran rampant. Many assumptions were made, but because of Lily's arrest a week later, some details about our relationship were revealed.

Those who paid attention to the news, or who listened to Lily's crazy rantings, were made privy to some of the details of our romance. While some were kind to Summer, others were not. But she remained strong, and finished the semester with grace.

Surprisingly, Serena was quite instrumental in acquiring the evidence needed against Lily. When she suspected it was Lily who sent the photos to the University and Summer, she made an impromptu visit to Lily's apartment. It was quite a revelation when Serena *happened* to stumble upon Summer's stolen bag from the night she was mugged, in Lily's bedroom closet. After one call to my friend Cameron, and some intense questioning by him while she was in custody, she was singing like a canary.

She'd been expelled by the school, ordered to serve ninety days for theft and assault, which was ultimately reduced to five days behind bars and then probation. One of the stipulations in her release, which Summer pleaded for, was that she receive mental health counseling. It was clear that was what she needed, not jail. And just another reason I loved my girl so much.

"Are you excited?" I ask the woman of my dreams who's currently fixated on the view outside the plane as we descend into Paris.

"I can't believe we're going to spend six months here!" Her eyes twinkle as she shines a bright smile my way before returning her focus to the window. "It's so beautiful." She points, the tip of her finger poking against the glass. "It's the Eiffel Tower!"

"I'll take you there for dinner, Princess." I squeeze her hand. "You'll love the view."

Yes, we're staying in the city of love for the next six months. I took a job as an adjunct professor at Dauphine University teaching a mathematics course for one semester. I only have three classes a week. Which will leave plenty of time for Summer and I to spend together.

She's taking the semester off. Her dream was to live,

see, and experience the world, and I want to help her do that. Share every moment I can with her. I pat the inside pocket of my jacket, reassuring myself that the diamond ring I purchased over a month ago is still safe.

I've wanted to ask her to marry me every day since I bought it. But I also don't want to rush her. I feel like our journey together has just begun. Forever waits for us, and putting this ring on her finger won't change that. I know she's mine. When the right moment presents itself, I'll be ready though.

The plane bounces several times as the wheels make contact with the runway, our bodies surging forward a bit as the pilot brakes.

"We're here!" She claps her hands with glee, bouncing in her seat. She's never been to Paris before.

Our story is just beginning, and I can't wait to show her the world.

And they lived happily ever after…
The End.

I really hope you enjoyed Alexender's story.
I would be so grateful if you could leave a review. It can be as simple as one sentence, but it makes such a difference in our books being seen. Thank you so very much!
https://geni.us/temptingteacher

If you liked the Tempting Series, take a look at my award winning series, The Auction Series. It's a billionaire, auction, dom-sub, secret identity love story that's full of twists that will keep you turning the pages.
The first book is called The Winning Bid and can be found here:
https://geni.us/winningbid

Acknowledgments

If you've made it this far, then my number one thank you goes to you, my reader. It's been quite awhile since I wrote and published a full-length book, and if you stuck around and waited for me, or if you're a new reader, I'm so truly grateful to you. You are the reason I write, and I hope this story allowed you to escape into a sexy, fun, alternate world for just a little while.

For a long time, I didn't know if I could or would ever write again. The end of a heartbreaking friendship, covid, and then a heart attack stalled my creativity, as well as my confidence. One cold week in February 2024, at a writing retreat hosted by one of my very dear friends, Lydia Michaels, changed all of that. The women that shared that week with me also shared their fears, their hopes, their dreams, but more importantly, their strength, their love, and their support. A full moon, sea-shelled intentions, conversations that fed my soul, and so many laughs left me renewed, and feeling like I could conquer the world. Or at least, write again. Lydia, Willow, DD, Sam, Mimi, Ellie, and Heather, thank you from the bottom of my heart for giving me life again.

I want to extend an extra special thank you to Lydia,

whom I also dedicated this book to. Your friendship, your belief in me, means more than I can ever express. You've shown me what true friendship is and should be, and I will treasure it, and you for eternity. Thank you for every phone call, text, evil clown picture, laugh we've shared, bitch session, your endless wealth of knowledge, and for sharing your heart. It's one of the best out there.

To my husband, Doug, thank you for supporting my dreams. For loving me. For hugging me when I need it. For all the amazing business advice. You are definitely the better half of this relationship and I'm so entirely blessed to have you as my partner.

Felicia, Tyler and Tommy, I love you more than there are stars in the sky. You'll always be my truest loves.

Mom, thanks for being my biggest fan, for passing down your love of reading, and for being someone I will always look up to and cherish.

Tammy, Laura, and Karla; more than my sisters. My best friends, my life blood, the soothing balm for my soul at any time. Espresso martini's soon!

A huge thank you to Cin Medley for being my biggest cheerleader and always, always at the ready when I need you. Love you so much!

Julie, Robin and Mindy, thank you for always supporting me and showing up to my signings. Love you girls to pieces.

Michelle Windsor is the author of over a dozen steamy, contemporary romances filled with alpha males and even stronger females. She has achieved both Amazon and Barnes & Noble International Best Seller status, and was awarded Best Contemporary Romance Writer by Passionate Plume Ink in 2019. Her first book, The Winning Bid, was nominated for the Summit Indie Book Awards by Metamorph Publishing in 2017, and continues to be her best-selling book to date.

Michelle is married with three grown children, and lives north of Boston in the type of suburban neighborhood you read about in sweet romance books, (not hers)! When she's not working on another book, you can find her spending time with her husband, hanging out with her three sisters, or snuggled up with her three cats, yes three, watching a movie or reading a book.

Keep up to date with Michelle on her web page:
https://www.authormichellewindsor.com